What W
Security

C000293087

A thought-provoking and business-focused look at problems and missed opportunities within Information Security.

For business and security leaders alike.

To moving mountains.

Table of Contents

Introduction

Welcome to this special first release of *What We Call Security*.

This is a book about information security, but one looking at things from a macro, human, and industry level rather than an academic or technical one.

This is atypical for "security", and the result of me perhaps being an atypical "security person". One who likes to think about how the big picture fits together.

For example, despite my current title of Chief Technologist (for Security) at CDW, I don't really care about technology.

I'll be honest with you; I don't get particularly excited about "security" either.

I'm far more interested in business and business outcomes. I'm passionate about driving efficiency, organisational culture, quality, the bottom line, potential, and people.

Here's the kicker: These things, in my opinion, generate better security too. Far better than the status quo focused almost exclusively on "security" technology, while also making it a tangible business contributor rather than an ambiguous cost centre.

And that's what this book is about. Having an honest (and at times brutal) look at why the current approach is failing and why I feel we need to approach things not just at a higher level, but also very differently.

Unlike most security books out there, this one is more about taking an executive view, giving a cultural critique, and doing some strategic ideation. Heck, in parts it's almost philosophical.

It highlights principles that, if taken in with an objective mind, I hope will resonate. Principles I hope some of you will adopt.

Note that it assumes some familiarity about current practices and the associated problems. Enough so that when I give analogies, things click.

On that note, it may be worthwhile to read my last book, *Rethinking InfoSec,* before (or after) reading this one.

While my thinking there was certainly less mature than in this book, when read together you may see some of its chapters in a new light and get greater a context of some of the issues I want to address here.

Neither book is comprehensive, not even close, but hopefully they can open up new avenues of thinking and spark ideas that will benefit you.

That is my main goal. If it can do that, then I would consider it a success.

Finally, yes, these are largely opinions. My opinions, based on my experience and results. Some of the stories and anecdotes have been slightly modified, mostly to protect the guilty.

Feel free to dismiss or ignore them, my only ask is that you be objective in doing so because some people much smarter than me, who have taken a step back and looked at things beyond the status quo, share them too.

On with the show.

Hitachi Vantara

I want to take a moment to thank Hitachi Vantara and the fantastic people there for supporting this project.

This book came along as part of a larger project to write a blog explaining the relevance of storage and recovery to a holistic, outcomes-focused, business security strategy.

As a foundational cornerstone, that series involved taking a broader, holistic view of what was and wasn't working in our industry. You'll find that blog series bundled at the back of this book In Appendix B. I promise some of the concepts we came up with are worth your time, especially those around risk management and remediation.

It is that work which then inspired this book. It is essentially a deeper dive into so many of the issues our industry faces, and which approaches could help us move forward.

I should add that the book is not specifically aimed at anything Hitachi Vantara does, nor did they provide me with any guidance or conditions on what this book should be about.

I feel this speaks to their commitment to helping make the world a better place and, on a more personal note, faith that I may be able to provide something towards that goal. For that I am thankful.

That said, working with them and thinking about storage from a security perspective has given me some ideas that could potentially change some very fundamental things in how we practice security.

Together we've come up with some ideas that I think can greatly empower us to shift to a more strategic and sustainable way of approaching security. I believe, after the perspectives offered in this book, you'll see just how important the role of some of their offerings could be.

I hope you enjoy reading that blog series at the end of this book and get value out of some of the concepts and approaches we came up with.

Audience

One of my most common challenges at CDW is to talk to the right people to help drive great outcomes for our customers.

As soon as they hear the word "security", I'm often invited to have a conversation with a Head of Information Security, a Security Architect, etc. Rarely a business leader.

But that is where the change must happen, and that's who this book is aimed at. Business leaders, and those CISOs who consider themselves business executives first and "security people" second, or at least want to progress in that direction.

There's nothing technical about this book. That's not because I'm catering to a largely non-technical audience, but rather because there's nothing fundamentally technical about *security*.

If anything, I feel the focus on technology distracts us from being able to see [and therefore address] the real problems. It also confuses the needed stakeholders and creates a lack of accountability for security practitioners, hiding them behind a confusing veil of technology.

I suggest instead that we step away from the nitty gritty of "security technology" and take a climb up to 35,000 feet in order to look at how the entire sector works, and how other industries have successfully solved analogous problems. Problems we have failed to even realise are analogous because we've had our face far too close to the ground.

As mentioned before, this book is aimed at present and aspiring security leaders, not technologists (though they may benefit). It is also aimed a more executive non-technical audience like the CEO, CFO, COO, and similar.

If you are a "security person" actually reading a non-technical book with a slant on leadership and strategy, then thank you. We need so many more of you if we're to solve the issues, the real ones, within our industry.

If you are a business leader who is *not* a "security person" taking an interest in what is going on in the world of security, wanting to learn what to look for in your security leaders, what good might look like in security, and how you can get business value out of security, I hope you enjoy and learn from this book.

We need you to be educated about the problem for you to hire and trust the right people, to put the right security leadership in place to solve your problems rather than perpetuate them.

I believe much of the messaging out there today is dangerously misleading in this area.

Part One – Setting the Stage

I recently saw a comment on LinkedIn that somewhat intimated what this book is about.

Someone had posted a quote from my first book, *Rethinking InfoSec*:

"The vast majority of InfoSec work is either finding and remediating known vulnerabilities or responding to incidents caused by their presence."

It was something I wrote about our status quo, and how silly it seemed to me that we allowed known issues into production environments. And when I say "known issues" I mean issues we've fundamentally known about for *twenty years or more*.

It's what leads security practitioners down an endless and ever-worsening firefighting crusade and, no matter how hard they try, ultimately leads to most breaches (in my experience). It's what I feel we need to change in order to stop the reactive rut we're currently stuck in.

Then came that comment:

"The challenge here is the age-old issue of ownership and priority. We don't own any of it, IT does, and their mission is focused on enabling the business through and only through availability and convenience, thus the persistence of the issue."

He was absolutely correct, with the possible exception that it's not just "IT".

So, while it certainly feels like a tiny minority, some of us *have* identified the root issue; we know we need to fix things upstream. The problem is we don't have ownership, so we can't.

Except we can.

To do so requires significant levels of business engagement, usually far outside the sphere of our place in the org chart and our defined responsibilities.

We must do it anyway, because until we fix the underlying problems all we are doing is delaying the inevitable, at best.

As such, this book is about three main things:

1. Openly discussing the issues within security. Not the technical stuff we like to talk about to make ourselves seem important, but our failures in taking that needed ownership and the ugly truths we don't want to admit, or even realise, that have allowed us to get to where we are today.

2. Presenting and exploring a more holistic, cumulatively effective, and cheaper approach to reducing risk (while driving many business benefits) by no longer focusing foremost on risk but something else entirely.

3. Driving an understanding of business and senior stakeholders as to better adapt our approach and communication to them and get traction from them. Also, how we can contribute to the business and bottom line to be part of the conversation at those levels.

This book is, in many ways, about making what many practitioners consider "impossible" possible by empowering ourselves to accomplish our and the business's goals, rather than just do "our jobs".

Let's set the stage by looking at where things stand today.

Trigger Warning

This part of the book doesn't provide the answers, we'll get to that later. For now, I just want us to think about the problem.

This will be harsh. It's also a generalisation and, to some degree, hyperbole (although some places are even worse that what I'll be laying out here). I also can't speak to every single security function and security leader out there, so please humour me.

None of what I am saying will apply to everyone. There will be degrees to each of these issues which will vary by organisation, team, and leadership.

I fervently hope that some people will disagree because they don't engage in the behaviours I'll be pointing out. That would indicate progress.

Others may disagree because they recognise themselves and go on the defensive. Fortunately, it's unlikely these people buy my books. Unfortunately, they're the ones we most need to help.

Luckily I've also been blessed and spurred on by the ones who, to quote someone who messaged me to comment about my previous book, "gave [themselves] whiplash from nodding so hard in agreement."

And then there is the comfort of knowing that some real heavyweights in our industry agree with me.

People like Drew Simonis, CISO at Juniper Networks and former Global VP of Cyber Security at HP Enterprise who recently replied to me on LinkedIn as follows:

I've long argued that the biggest barrier to security is the security team. We can't stand to solve a problem, preferring lots of ongoing operations instead. In brief, we are a massive symptom management function.

[With a] huge conflict of interest or at least the perception of one... how do you grow your empire if you are eliminating root causes as we both agree we need to?

Why doesn't everyone agree with us here?!?!?

This section is just meant to be food for thought, my attempt at a frank exposé on the issues in our industry and our profession.

How those who want to fix them can do so is either self-evident, or something I hope to address later in the book.

To a Hammer, Everything Looks Like a Nail

We've all heard the expression that, to a hammer, everything looks like a nail.

In *Rethinking InfoSec*, I gave an analogy about the security industry as follows:

Imagine your main electrical junction box at home blows up. You call an electrician, obviously.

They carefully examine the box for some time and determine it needs to be completely replaced as it's toast. They do so and the power is back.

A week later it blows up, again. You call them, again. They replace it, again.

A week after that it blows up, again. You call them, again.

This time they suggest spending a little more money on a beefier model. It blows up again, but after a month rather than a week.

Ah! Result! It lasted four times longer than the last one.

So, we decide to go bigger still. The bigger [and even more expensive] model lasts a full three months! Let's scale up some more!

After a few iterations you end up with a massive, cumbersome, and very expensive industrial junction box in your house, but it only blows up once a year.

At some point afterward your sink gets clogged, so you call a plumber.

The plumber, naturally, can't help but notice the enormous junction box taking up half your kitchen wall.

Five seconds later they turn to you and ask: "How long has that water pipe up there been leaking onto the junction box?"

This analogy captures two major points about our problem in making security work. They are so closely related that you could argue they are the same, but I'll keep them separate for now as to address them later more easily.

1. Our belief that Information Security is fundamentally a technology problem.
2. How that myopic vision of the problem space leads to the wrong "solutions."

Worse still is that we propagate these notions to others, implying it's something "very technical" that "normal people" can't understand, when we, the "security people" are possibly the ones looking at the problem wrong.

It also means we're biased in who we hire (What electrician firm would hire a plumber?), often excluding the very people most able to help improve things. For our organisations and the world.

We talk about a cybersecurity skills gap in our industry, claiming millions more are needed globally, and yet every time I need to build a team, I manage to rapidly recruit groups of exceptional individuals able to outperform just about anyone in their ability to reduce an organisation's risk, without the help of recruiters, and at below-market salaries.

These are people that understand the organisational, business, and human context, with the ability to influence real change, not affected by tech or "cyber" myopathy.

The irony? Most have been told over and over that they're not qualified or not sufficiently experienced, even for entry level positions. Because they're "not technical enough".

The ones that get a chance tend to progress on to exceptional careers, rapidly overtaking the very people who genuinely believed they were not qualified. They tend to do it via a variety of roads, with the commonality of them being the roads less travelled.

But before discussing this further, let's have a high-level look at how Security is doing.

The Trend

I'm frequently asked what the trends are in cyber security.

What new technologies should companies be buying, what should vendors and resellers be pitching and selling, what game changing tech is around the corner.

My answer? I don't know, nor do I really care. I feel most industry chatter about these things misses the bigger picture completely.

There's only one trend in security I care about. Ok, let's say two but I feel that they are related:

SIZE OF GLOBAL CYBER SECURITY MARKET WORLDWIDE ($ billion)

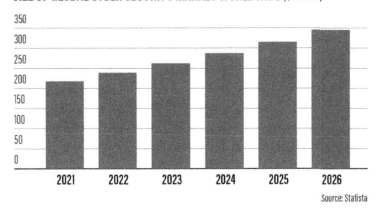

Source: Statista

Every single year we spend more money on cyber security. Significantly more.

And...

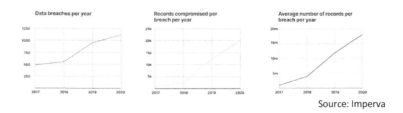

Source: Imperva

Every single year things get worse. Significantly worse.

I know the years on these charts don't line up, but it doesn't matter. You can find hundreds of these graphs about the security market using google and the trends are the same.

And while resellers and cyber security companies love this as it means that it's a growing market (graph 1), which can only keep growing (graph 2), I think it's wrong.

It's morally wrong, and we should be embarrassed about it – as practitioners – because we're not only not fixing the problem, but we're also placing a burden on our organisations who are paying us to do so.

The simple fact is that if you're addressing a problem correctly, certainly after spending hundreds of billions on it over an extended period (I'd say the "modern" approach to security has been around a couple of decades now), you expect to see some results, not for things to get worse.

Some might argue that we have more and more systems and organisations out there, but I would counter that with the fact that the percentage of them implementing some form of "security technology" is higher than ever, and that "incidents" (we'll look at the relevance of this later) in other industries are down significantly over the same period despite those industries having grown substantially.

Others will point out that the number of threats is forever increasing and that's why we can't keep up. To them I'd respond that *we* are potentially fuelling that growth in the number of threat actors due to the sheer number of easy opportunities we leave for them to exploit.

Quite bluntly, it is my belief that the cyber security industry, for the most part, does not address the causes of our problems.

And what it does do even indirectly encourages the problem to get worse.

To illustrate this in a simple analogy:

Imagine someone stores bags of grain in their garden, and one day wakes up to find thousands of mice everywhere.

My job is to keep the environment mouse-free.

What do I do?

Let's start with some simple questions:

23

Do I have a mouse problem? Or a grain storage problem?

The answer is yes, to both. But one is probably causing the other, or at least aggravating it enormously.

The next thing to realise is that attacking the mouse problem by itself is all but hopeless. You will spend an absolute fortune on mousetraps, lose huge amounts of time, and you still won't get anywhere near all of them.

Then there's the fact that the problem will probably still reproduce faster than you can buy more mousetraps and it'll get worse than ever the second you stop or take a break.

Conversely, changing how we store our bags of grain would likely result in a rapid drop in the mouse population, to a level where a handful of traps would be enough to mop up the odd mouse.

All this to say that improving how we operate our business and IT processes will drive far better security than firefighting the result of poor practices.

But that's bad news for the mousetrap industry.

Practitioner Bias

One of the things I find most peculiar about how we practice information security today is just how unaware a lot of practitioners, including ones in managerial and leadership roles, are about the sheer ineffectiveness of what we're doing... and how steadfast they are in their belief that doing more of it will help.

In fact, many vendors and practitioners drown us in FUD-based marketing (That stands for Fear, Uncertainty, and Doubt – Yes, we have an actual term for it.) to scare us into buying more products and services by using the very trends caused by narrow-mindedly using their products and services.

I once gave a presentation to a group of CISOs here in the UK where I showed two unlabelled graphs, both very simple with just two lines on them.

The first showed a line going upwards along the horizontal axis, a second also going up similarly although slightly faster.

I said this graph showed the gun ownership rate per capita in the United States and the murder rate per capita in the United States.

There was a bit of a chuckle from the audience, and you could almost hear the "Well duh! Stupid Americans with their guns. Obviously."

The second graph meanwhile showed one line going up along the horizontal axis, much like in the previous graph, but with a second line starting at the top and going down along the horizontal axis, almost the inverse of the first.

I said this line showed the representation between investment in cyber security (spending/security budgets) and the impact (frequency and scale) of breaches.

People nodded in agreement, looking at each other with proud smiles, giving themselves a pat on the back.

Of course, this is what they were here for. This was their job and why they did it.

And then I told them I switched the graphs.

Silence.

I did this for dramatic effect, to drive a point home.

(To their credit they did eventually have a good laugh and paid very close attention to the rest of the presentation. A great audience.)

I've already shared some security macro trends in the previous chapter, but I'd like us to look at the ones about the gun ownership and murder rates.

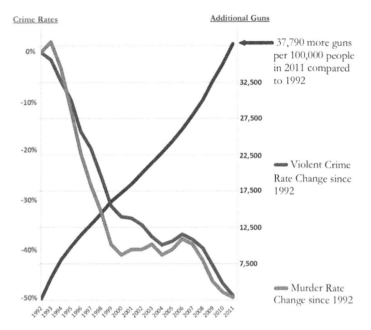

Crime Rates   **Additional Guns**

37,790 more guns per 100,000 people in 2011 compared to 1992

Violent Crime Rate Change since 1992

Murder Rate Change since 1992

Additional guns (net of exports) from United States Department of Justice Bureau of Alcohol, Tobacco, Firearms and Explosives: Firearms Commerce in the United States Annual Statistical Update 2013
Crime Rates & Population Data from the FBI website: http://www.fbi.gov/about-us/cjs/ucr/crime-in-the-u.s/2011/crime-in-the-u.s.-2011/tables/table-1

I find it very interesting how people assume, even expect, the opposite, and I like to share it for several reasons:

1. It makes people uncomfortable because it's a touchy subject. This is a good thing. We need to not shy away from controversy to appreciate all factors and make the best decisions.

2. Cognitive dissonance. Most people expect the opposite and have adopted ideologies to that effect. We have to improve our openness to accept facts, especially when they disagree with us. That's growth. We need lots of that in our

industry! Ideological bias needs to be shaken apart. Such biases are absolutely present in the practice of security.

3. It shows us that the simplistic assumption of "guns kill people" (which is about the same as "spoons make people fat") and the associated equation of "more guns equal more gun violence" *and vice versa* is wrong.

    It's a highly complex situation. There are countries with vastly lower gun ownership rates and far higher gun violence rates and vice versa. Within countries there are cities, and neighbourhoods within those cities, with wildly different outcomes despite the measured input metrics being the same. Why?

    We must look at the whole of many, *many* complex factors to understand the why, otherwise we may make things worse.

    Alternatively, we may only need to identify potentially much simpler but accurate indicators or correlations. As a silly example, we may find that processed cheese consumption rates may map more tightly to murder rates than gun numbers. You never know, it all depends on what cause them and they may have commonalities that make one a good indicator of the other under certain circumstances

For example, I tell cyber insurers to look not at the presence (or lack) of security controls, but rather at the quality of business processes, as the primary measure of a customer's likelihood to experience a breach.

The presence of many controls may even be a negative factor, indicating there is an inability to address issues at source and requiring more compensating controls.

More on that later.

4. In our field, this simplistic "guns kill people" assumption manifests itself with people pushing for more of an approach that, at a high level anyway, has been proven to fail. We inevitably find that these approaches were chosen due an incomplete and insufficient scope of thinking about the problem.

5. There are factors, such as deterrence, which are much harder to quantify. They're also much harder to *sell* emotionally. One person dying is far more likely to cause a knee-jerk call for action than ten people having deterred lethal violence by being armed (which didn't make the news).

In security we make fanfare whenever someone is breached claiming it's because they didn't have X. We blame them for not having X and yet say nothing about others that have excellent track records despite not having X. Meanwhile, when someone who did have X gets breached, we claim the reason is that they didn't have *enough* X.

It's a catch 22 for accountability, and people chase this logic round ad nauseum instead of looking for the real underlying causes.

6. "Social" (or business/cultural) dynamics are likely to be, fundamentally, both the cause and the solution. In fact, the guns, or the security threats, likely aren't even the real problem. And we're largely ignoring them.

Then there is the possibility that policies and approaches put into action in an effort to improve the problem can, in reality, exacerbate it.

That sometimes, the person responsible for introducing that wrong solution, making things worse, is us.

And that we won't truly be able to solve the problem we claim to be fighting until we fix ourselves first.

Part Two – How Did We Get Here?

So, we've had a look at the trends. They're obviously not very good.

In fact, it's so obvious that we should have noticed it by now and come up with something better, so what gives?

I'm not going to sugar-coat it, the next 40 or so pages are one big rant about a lot of the more human, cultural, organisational, political, and mindset problems I see in the industry.

They, more than anything else in this book, will reflect my personal experience... and perhaps my own special brand of cynicism (though always with the hope of positive change).

I don't pretend to have all the answers to these problems and behaviours, but we should at least be honest about what we do for those we claim to serve.

The people trusting us as practitioners have a right to know so that they can select the right people and approaches to achieve the outcomes they deserve.

I hope most of you will be able to relate somewhat on at least some of these points.

A Strange Devolution

My perception is that 25 years ago, the way of making things secure was still to develop them properly with good architecture and well-thought-out code, good processes, and so on.

Weirdly, we've rather stopped doing this.

We've instead moved to a model where we shore up defects with ever-fancier new technological bandages, rather than addressing what caused them.

So, what happened?

Well, part of it is likely down to increasing pressure to up the speed of innovation, development, and deployment.

But the security industry is arguably also responsible to some degree by positioning security as a separate function or department and inadvertently *creating* the perception in other departments (and in management teams) that security isn't their responsibility.

This saw very little objection from the security industry as it meant huge growth in the market to mitigate an ever-increasing number of issues. The outputs from various departments became less and less innately secure, requiring more and more additional layers of security controls and staff to monitor and operate them.

The strength of the financial driver here shouldn't be underestimated. One only needs to look at the amount of VC spend and [hyper]valuations on cyber security companies over the last few years.

Afterall, why fix fundamental issues when *not* fixing them creates ever-increasing opportunities to sell new "solutions" and services?

Perhaps more worrying is that, after a decade or more of this messaging, it seems to have almost completely taken the focus away from what's causing the security concerns in the first place.

This has not just been detrimental to businesses' overall level of assurance but has also gotten all of us into a firefighting spiral from which it is becoming increasingly difficult to escape.

The Accountability Problem

There's something peculiar about how we practice security today. An unintended result or, if you're cynical, a fringe benefit for practitioners:

There's not much accountability.

You didn't get hacked today (though you didn't actually do anything)?

Good job.

You *did* get hacked but you've been so remiss in your duties that you haven't even noticed?

Er... Good job, still, I guess?

You've been comprehensively and publicly handed your own backside through an issue or combination of issues you'd not identified and weren't even on a trajectory to *eventually* identify resulting in grievous harm to your organisation?

Oh dear. Surely that's just a prime example of "It's not a matter of if but when"? You poor thing.

We could be asking some questions about the efficacy of our past investment in security, but how about we let you hire three more people and give you a bigger budget instead?

I'm obviously being facetious but, in some cases, not by much. Not at all.

What other part of a business would get this kind of leeway?

A few years back I was at an event where attending senior executives from various companies were asked why they funded their information security functions.

Do you know what the most common answer was?

"To make them go away."

Most of the other answers, when questioned, ultimately came down to "We don't really understand it (information security), but we're told we have to do it."

They were never sold on the value by their own security functions. They essentially had them only because they were told they should.

I can't think of any other business department that would be allowed to exist or continue operating that way.

We have created a perception about our industry that what we do is so technical, so geeky, so complicated, that no one else can understand it... and that it makes us special, "elite", important.

The reality is that, as a result, "normal" people, which includes everyone from mail clerks to executives, don't *want* to understand it. And they don't want to deal with *us*.

One consequence of this phenomenon, rather conveniently for some, is that it shields us from accountability because no one else can understand what we're supposed to do, what good looks like for us, and how to measure our results.

This is compounded by a track record of poor communication, and sometimes even hostile or dismissive attitudes, that makes people not want to talk to security teams in the first place.

What should be seen as unacceptable or poor performance is tolerated as "needed" under this veil of "cyber" that most people don't understand.

I used to audit companies post breach for cyber insurers. Do you know how many times I was successful at showing negligence by their security teams?

Every single time. Within hours of walking through the door.

This level of performance shouldn't be acceptable.

Don't get me wrong, security is hard to do well, it takes years to roll out an effective programme.

But when I see CISOs and security teams that have been in place for years who don't have a strategy, a programme, or a roadmap that would at least have *eventually* led to them discovering and addressing the issue that got them breached, then we have a real problem.

They were either just coasting and going to be relying on the "it's not if but when" excuse when it would finally go wrong, or so incredibly disconnected from reality that they actually thought they were doing an effective job.

The fact that none of those companies' management teams challenged the findings tells me they too didn't think those teams were doing a great job. Not once they'd read the report anyway.

We in security have created the very silo we so often complain about being stuck in, yet we seem to do little to get out of it. Maybe because we know we'd be accountable if we did.

But accountability is essential if we are to work out and drive approaches that work.

Altruism

I recently, at time of writing anyway, shared a post on LinkedIn about the difference between a £120k CISO and a £180k-plus CISO where I added my thoughts.

For context, here in the UK, £120k tends to be the salary range where companies try to get someone to fill the CISO title as a tick in the box role, or one where they don't realise the business value of a "real" C-level CISO thinking it's just a gloried Security Manager or Head of Security Operations, whereas £180k is where you start having real strategic roles where the companies are serious enough to pay the money.

The practical difference between the two, in my opinion, is a lot of business value. Mostly in the form of general business and leadership savvy.

Quoting from it here:

£120k CISO sets up/manages [IT] security operations.

£180k CISO is a lot more likely to understand your business (kind of important) and can help you understand how to secure it. But, just from a money standpoint, he/she...

-continuously streamlines your operational security costs by tens or hundreds of thousands per year.

-negotiates significant savings on solutions, saving you tens or hundreds of thousands per year.

-finds and trains better talent at lower rates while needing fewer recruiters, saving you tens or hundreds of thousands per year.

-improves business process throughout the business saving you hundreds of thousands per year on operating costs in other departments too.

-commercialises your security as a brand value and adds commercial propositions that land you hundreds of thousands or more of additional business per year.

-is orders of magnitude more likely to address the risks that will actually hurt you due to understanding the business context.

-will drive cumulative and *lasting* improvements by changing your business processes rather than firefighting issues resulting from them, further lowering your security costs over time.

The cheap option isn't cheap.

There's a lot of added value which makes that extra £60k in payroll an absolute bargain.

And notably a lot of it comes not just business savvy as I mentioned before, but also out of a sense of *altruism to the business.*

I do personally feel that falls under leadership "skills", but not everyone defines leadership the way I do so I felt it worthwhile to mention it separately.

That altruism, that desire to contribute, and even a certain concern about whether we are contributing *enough* is something I don't see a lot of in our industry.

Let's be honest. There is a level of feel-good virtue in being a security practitioner.

You need only go to a cyber security conference to hear practitioners talk about how important they are, always saving the day for everyone. (Don't get me started on all our industry awards for... having done what exactly?)

In some ways, I guess there's nothing fundamentally wrong with that. A little reward for a job well done is good, and ego can be a great motivator when channelled properly.

But I can't help but feel that a lot of the claims we make fall flat when we must justify them to outsiders.

How sure are we, *really*, that we are making a tangible benefit to the organisation?

Let me ask something even more fundamental:

How truly do we believe in our cause?

If I could make all our information security problems disappear by snapping my fingers, how many security practitioners would say go ahead?

If you offered a soldier to end a war in this way, they would say yes, without a second thought. Would we?

Security practitioners should ask themselves the same question and be honest about the answer.

Are we even incentivised to fix the problem when we can get in-demand low accountability six-figure jobs for keeping it going under the veil that "it's complicated"?

I have seen first-hand how this can drive behaviour that is counterproductive to security, by security practitioners themselves. I've seen analysts drum up reports, and I've seen CISOs shoot down initiatives that would bring visibility and possibly accountability.

I'm willing to bet many readers that have been around the block will be able to think of a case or two where they saw similar behaviour.

Most plumbers, electricians, builders, lawyers, accountants, etc. don't deliberately perform poorly to ensure they have repeat business.

To the contrary, they do a *good* job, which creates value to their customers, and more work opportunities find them as a result.

Now I'm not saying security practitioners are, as a majority, deliberately *not* securing things to ensure job security, but the current approach does produce similar dynamics.

For example, ask yourself whether the main force behind the huge demand for security practitioners is because they provide great value and ROI, or because there's a problem elsewhere that keeps getting worse that demands security bodies to mitigate?

Security bodies which are not, in most cases, fundamentally addressing that problem, and who do not really generate *tangible* value [for the business] on their own.

This needs to change. And that means we need to change. We cannot claim to be contributing selflessly to our organisations until we do, nor will we drive our true potential value for which we will be most appreciated.

Fixing the approach so that we *permanently* resolve a lot of the issues in what we build going forward won't leave us high and dry. It just means we'll have to evolve to create value rather than firefight. And there will still be *plenty* of mopping up work for us to do while we make that transition.

And if that doesn't make sense yet, just keep reading, we'll get there.

Burning Money

The altruism conversation leads me to another, related one: security budgets and spending.

Years ago, I wrote an article entitled "Burn Your Money" off the back of seeing a CISO's resume where the first line highlighted his ability to get businesses to increase their security spending.

In that article I talked about how much money is spent on technical tooling (often implemented ineffectively), how much resource that tied up for poor results, and how it promoted ever more focus on the security tools used to detect and respond to incidents rather than on addressing the IT and business processes that were leading to them in the first place.

I suggested that one of the best things you could do to improve your security was to freeze your security spending for six months or more.

I reckoned that after the initial screaming, outrage, and thumb twiddling, security teams would eventually get up, walk around, and see what they could do.

These things might include:

- Addressing long-overdue missing patches and the reasons why patching was ineffective in the first place.

- Creating an effective naming scheme to better understand systems.
- Update asset inventories to see what systems they're currently not covering.
- Build relationships with other departments to have open lines of communications.
- Create standards around system builds and hardening to reduce issues over time.
- Do access reviews, fix issues with access, and create processes for access to be issued correctly going forward.
- Finish deploying or correctly configuring the tools they already have.
- Systematically going through systems and applications to ensure they were configured correctly and define standards to be followed by IT going forward.
- Reviewing business processes to better understand security risks.
- Define processes and standards wherever possible that would result in other departments producing fewer security concerns.

And so on and so forth. In short, addressing all the basic issues leading to most of the incidents they were having to firefight today, and a few policies and processes to stop new ones from being introduced.

The number of memes I see in security circles about management being stupid because they won't allocate security a bunch of money (likely because security has been unable to articulate the business value), and how the security team is suddenly flush with cash after a breach (possibly caused by their own failure to address some of the no- and low-cost actions listed above) irks me to no end. I'm embarrassed to be associated with that profession.

This applies to both tooling and team sizes and causes yet another problem around the hiring of security leadership.

I've observed that many security leadership positions have criteria like size of budget and teams led.

For example, a job description will indicate they want someone who's had teams of 20+ people and managed an operational budget of £5,000,000+ per year.

According to those qualifications, a candidate who's been able to deliver significantly better results with a staff of six and a third of the spending, because they thought and acted more cleverly, strategically, or altruistically, would be dismissed from consideration for not being "senior" enough.

In fact, the more wasteful and inefficient a security leader is in a given scenario, the more senior they'll be considered according to these worryingly common hiring standards. Again, partially because we've gotten away with doing a job in a way no one understands for so long.

The lack of altruism and accountability mentioned in previous chapters play a significant role here, but it's also important for hiring managers to be well informed and dictate the kinds of security leadership being hired.

Long story short: If you are a senior leader in your business and you do not have a clear understanding of what your security department does and what business value it delivers, please do not let the incumbent set the hiring criteria on their own and do not make them a decision maker. It's a recipe for poor effectiveness and high security spend.

[Lack of] Competency Bias

I once worked for a start-up where the product engineering department was, let's say, a mess.

There didn't seem to be any organisation, the output per head was conspicuously low, turnover was high, the quality of the work was downright *dangerous* both in terms of us using it internally and from the legal liability of our clients using it.

Even our Head of Sales, when presented with insights into the state of our product (which wasn't limited to security issues), said "We can't sell this." (There may have been a more colourful preamble.)

How did we get there? Well, fundamentally, it was a culture and hiring problem.

When the company was founded, an engineer was hired. Let's say the son of a friend of the founder. He produced something that, functionally, seemed to do what the founder wanted.

And when the company expanded as more potential customers showed interest, this engineer was told to hire more people. What then happened was down to the fact that he saw himself as a techie and he wasn't about to hire other techies that were better than him or could provide better direction than him.

So, whereas an experienced leader would have stepped away from the work, looked at what the business needed, and hired the best darn people he or she could find in order to execute, all this techie did was hire more techies, mostly ones that we're less experienced than him. The result on culture, competence, and outcomes was inevitable.

This also happens in security. *A lot*.

I've seen it in interviews, I've been demoted for taking initiative, I've been fired after clients requested I be promoted, and I am not alone.

Conversations and warnings about not overperforming one's manager or company status quo have come up frequently during my career and those of fellow altruistic practitioners.

Solving problems is disruptive and threatening to those maintaining that status quo.

The field of information security may be particularly susceptible to this phenomenon due to the lack of understanding by senior leadership teams as to what security functions do and how they should ideally be operating (what good looks like).

As a result, bad leaders, from middle managers up to CISOs, can remain in place a very long time.

Not a week goes by where I don't hear of someone in my network leaving because they are fed up with their boss.

It's often the ones I rate highly who were hired "by accident". Their managers then start finding them "troublesome" once they start doing the things the business needs rather than what their manager wants.

I fear there are a lot of such bad leaders in our industry, and that means many of them have built bad teams. Teams that underperform, don't question, and don't take initiative.

This means that if you as a business leader want to drive change in your security function you may not just need new security leadership, you may need a whole new team.

It's my experience that CIOs taking the reins and getting more involved in security after a CISO leaves, sometimes after a breach or other event that brought attention onto the security team, often realise that the people they've inherited are their biggest challenge.

The tragic thing is that many of them might have had a lot of promise, but it was killed by poor leadership.

Sometimes it can be revived, but sometimes it's too late.

And that's not just a personal loss for them, but a loss and potentially even a burden to our whole profession.

Toxicity

Continuing from the previous chapter, while on one hand we have a lack of business-focus, leadership competency, and altruism in security, on another we sometimes have full-on toxicity.

And it is not limited solely to leadership roles.

I've seen a significant number of technical experts, truly savvy in their area, actively mock, denigrate, and ridicule anyone advocating alternative approaches, taking a more holistic view, or merely just asking questions.

Comments full of insults and clown face emojis are not uncommon within the security community on LinkedIn, belittling anyone questioning the technical elitists' status quo. (I'm glad to report significant improvement, but possibly only due to my fondness for the block function.)

And that's towards fellow security practitioners, often genuinely trying to help within the scope of their ability.

I have lost count of the number of times I have seen security practitioners, when in a meeting room by themselves, belittle users, managers, and company leadership. Security teams "not playing nicely with other departments" is a frequent comment I get from CIOs and other CxOs.

The irony of this arrogance is that many of these practitioners probably weren't providing much value for this very reason; a sense of entitlement and little interest in truly helping the business or its people.

These practitioners should have been sacked long ago, but many survived in post for years due to that enduring veil of "it's complicated", complicit security leaders, and the industry messaging that these individuals are somehow *so* important.

Marketing people are also important, so are Salespeople, so are Operations people, and so are many others across your organisation.

You still fire them when they don't perform. And, hopefully, you fire them when they are toxic.

Culture is important to me. We in security should be contributing, helping, and promoting cultures of fairness, accountability, altruism, support, understanding, and working towards shared goals, together.

I believe these things to be absolutely fundamental. We, possibly more than any other business function, need everyone to care and contribute, often in ways they may not deem to be "their responsibility", and so we should be leading by example.

After all, organisational culture is possibly the most critical thing to the success of a security programme.

We cannot tolerate toxic and unaccountable security practitioners and behaviours that would damage that culture.

Tech vs Business Mindset

I want to touch on the disconnect between tech (where most security people are in terms of mindset and culture) and business.

It's important to remind ourselves that most of us work for a business, where our job should be to support business goals.

I can't help but feel like many of us in security are not doing that. Most of us are not even *thinking* about doing that.

The conversations I hear at security events tend to have a level of geekiness that is hard to convey. But they are also focused almost exclusively on security tech, and usually on whichever is being hyped up at the time. If other things are being discussed, they're rarely if ever about business.

These events are full of fast-paced, impassioned discussions that you can often stun instantly with one simple question:

"How does that help the bottom line?"

All of a sudden, there's a pause, usually followed by people looking at each other, wondering if someone has an answer.

But I will usually, eventually, get an answer. Sometimes I even get this answer quite quickly.

And that answer is, more often than not, something along the lines of… "That's not our job, our job is risk."

I have news for them: I'm willing to bet their employer, at the senior-most level anyway, disagrees.

I'm sorry for being harsh about this, but for all the talk in security that we should have a seat at the big table, the fact is most practitioners, most people with the title "CISO", don't even know what they talk about there, let alone speak the language.

And if a CFO walked into the last cybersecurity practitioner's event I attended, I doubt they'd even make it to the bar before turning around and walking out.

I frequently argue that, when it comes to security, traction is more important than budget.

I can think of several scenarios where a £1 budget with full support from the business would have achieved more than a siloed tech-focused security function could with £1,000,000. And I'd have change left over for a soda.

We need business traction, and many security functions are not only detached from said business, but actively ignoring it. Even pushing it away.

Security vs IT Technology

Following on from the focus on technology at the expense of the business reality, I want to share another observation about the focus on "security" technologies in particular.

Many technologies have impacts on security. For example, your average SaaS application will have various authentication mechanisms, user profiles, APIs that require securing.

And yet, I rarely see security teams focus on them because they're not "security" tools or platforms.

Even more fundamental are elements of "IT Operations" that are critical to security but often ignored by security teams for the same reasons.

Let's use asset visibility and control as just one example.

When I start somewhere as a CISO, one of the very first things I need is full visibility and control over the environment. I need to know what systems we have, what's on them, what versions, how they are configured, and much more. I need to have a high confidence that I can see all the systems I need to protect and what state they are in, that the information is current (as close to real-time as possible), and that I can query and control those assets if I need to. Only then can I identify and rectify issues.

Without this level of control and visibility, it's essentially pointless to proceed with most other kinds of controls.

My personal experience has been that the actual numbers of assets is 10% to 20% higher than what IT has in their asset registers.

And much of the information in those asset registers or CMDBs (Configuration Management Databases) is often out of date.

As such, in an organisation of 20,000 assets there are likely 2,000 or more unmanaged assets. And that's not including the "managed" where I don't have a clear or current picture.

That's thousands of systems where security agents and monitoring won't be applied, that won't be subject to hardening processes, that won't be decommissioned properly, that won't be scoped for backup and recovery, that won't be audited, etc.

More importantly, I likely can't trust anything I see or am given by other departments in spreadsheets. If I can't get full visibility then I can't query, I can't apply the changes I need, I can't see if others have done so for me, and I basically have no confidence.

That's why putting that capability in place is often the first thing I do. And I'm always baffled at how many security practitioners look at me funny because "that's not security".

IT teams' priority is typically functional delivery. But it's security that requires a much higher level of granularity both in visibility and control. It's us that need the best IT management possible. Detail-focused quality IT is paramount to security.

The fact that many security practitioners don't think that these IT capabilities are absolutely essential to increase the level of security of an organisation frankly blows my mind.

A lack of IT quality creates countless ways for "security" controls to be circumvented or omitted. Insufficiently managed systems act like stones on the surface of a moat, allowing attackers to walk right over the top of our defences.

And yet I rarely see security teams focus on these issues because the solutions needed aren't "security" tools, and therefore it's not "security" work. Ironically completely undermining any possibility of holistic and thereby effective security.

The fundamentals matter, they are fundamental. But they rarely wear the banner of "security". That shouldn't mean we ignore them.

Scope of Thought

The solutions we end up thinking up and applying often depend on the perspective and scope with which we see the problem we're trying to solve.

The funny thing is we don't tend to know or realise that our scope is limited, because we just don't know any better.

Many practitioners are doing the best job they believe possible. And genuinely put in a lot of effort doing so.

But their impact is minimised, and fleeting, because they're not yet considering the whole picture.

Personally, I started my career thinking about things purely from a mainstream "cyber security" angle. When I then started considering the bigger picture of IT, it was a revelation. I felt like a truly holistic practitioner.

But I then started understanding business process and had the same epiphany. And then I started understanding leadership which allowed me to better lead people, which was life changing. And then I started understanding human factors, and then I started understanding economics, marketing, sales, and eventually the business or executive mindset.

Each time, a new world opened up and allowed me to tackle the problem more holistically, more effectively, more sustainably.

The problem I often see in our industry is that this isn't happening. I don't know if it's dogma, inertia, cognitive dissonance, a lack of critical thinking, an inability to engage or communicate (and therefore work) with people from other departments, tech myopathy, or all of the above.

But the result is that most practitioners go further and further down the rabbit hole of technology rather than down a path of holistic consideration.

The unfortunate thing is that there seems to be resistance to do anything else. Business, [good] strategy, soft skills, leadership, understanding of other parts of business, and more are mostly readily dismissed as not relevant by so many practitioners. They are rarely sought after in candidates too.

Even the ones that agree that much of their work or even just a particular issue comes from somewhere else more often than not respond with "That's not my job though." or, "but I don't own that." Rather than making it their job to go own it and address the issue for the benefit of all.

And, to repeat myself, I feel we get away with this due to the lack of understanding of "security" (something we perpetuate), which leads to us having little accountability.

The only question to me is how deliberate this is, and how much we allow it to lead us in the wrong direction.

Framework Obsession

Popping over to the GRC (Governance, Risk, & Compliance) side of the house for a moment, I want to highlight what I feel is an overreliance on third party frameworks, possibly as a continuation from the lack of business understanding we just discussed.

Most security teams today build their security functions according to a framework written by a third party that's never seen the business in question.

And while these typically have some latitude in adapting their methodologies and controls to the business, this usually results them in being adapted to *some* of the business' *IT*, and not the business itself. (Not to mention usually being applied very far downstream against technical problems rather than their true root causes.)

The result is a lack of alignment and coverage that usually yields poor assurance. Things are left out of scope, and the failure to address the root causes in the business creates workload issues that almost guarantee things that did fall in scope will still get missed.

But the culture of tick-box compliance this approach has led to is possibly the biggest problem of all.

Consider my analogy for this around an end of year school exam:

During the school year you are given a 500-page book on a given subject, on which there will be an exam at the end of the year.

You do not know what the exam questions will be, so you systematically go through every single part of the book to make sure you've covered anything you might need to know.

Third-party compliance (E.g.: ISO27001) audits are the opposite. You know exactly what the questions will be, and you only need to provide one good answer to each.

The result is that you go look at the 5% or so of the book you need to give a satisfactory answer to the questions you know will be asked, any more would be a waste of time.

The result is that you score 100%, but you've only covered 5% of the book.

You've only covered 5% of the ways your organisation could be breached. On top of that, even within that 5% you likely haven't addressed dependencies, the real-world effectiveness of controls, and other things that are critical if you don't want attackers to waltz around your defences.

Many orgs have compliance projects where security teams are tasked to get compliant. Once they are compliant, the next task, by their own admission, is to get secure.

In other words, resource that could have been spent securing the business was reallocated elsewhere: Tickbox compliance. In the name of security.

Worse still, the fact that the organisation is then compliant promotes the idea that they are secure. This isn't just misleading to all those they're doing business with but also tends to kill internal support for the security team to go out and *actually* try to secure stuff.

That's the irony: you end up with situations where compliance took resource away from security, and then made it much more difficult for those people to implement real security.

In my eyes, back to the school analogy, we must read the book. Our approach to compliance should be to go through and understand every business process and then define what good (which includes secure) looks like for each.

That defined good state is then what we should aspire to comply to. Not some arbitrary, ill-fitting, usually partially implemented, and IT-focused standard from someone that knows nothing about us.

The added bonus of doing it this way is that you are far more likely pass any test. Whether that be from an auditor for any given certification, or an attacker.

Diversity Disqualification

A funny thing has happened to me over the years.

When I first started out, I had little experience, certainly not what I would call well-rounded experience.

I made up for this by reading. I learned a lot about a lot, from books, about things I'd never done in practice.

I would then go to interviews and answer questions with whatever academic answers were in those books.

And I would get hired, consistently. If I had two interviews, it was pretty much a guarantee I'd be offered a job, probably two.

After a few years though, I started learning from the real world. And being one of those annoying people that likes to question and find different ways to do things, I had worked out that a lot of the academic things in those books didn't work very well. Some didn't work *at all* and others could be done differently to much better effect.

This had an unintended effect: I started to struggle to find work.

I was no longer giving the "correct" book answers to pass competency questions.

I was doing something different, something "diverse".

This leads me to another observation about the industry over the last few years which is that there is a significant push to increase "diversity".

The specific argument I hear in security that I am taking issue with the one where people state that we have a daunting problem, and more diversity will lead to new ideas in solving it.

Now, personally, I have a problem labelling human beings and their infinite individuality according to some arbitrary categories that have nothing to do with said individuality.

But I could not agree more about the importance of bringing in fresh thinking and perspectives to get those new ideas in. Thinking you might find in people with different life experiences, different backgrounds, different professions, different industries, different ways of working, different cultures, and different personalities.

But here's the kicker: After talking, writing, and waxing lyrical about the importance of diversity in security, what I see time and time again is that we turn down anyone that isn't doing things exactly the way we've been doing them, in the same way I started being rejected for roles once I'd figured out better approaches that deviated from the status quo.

We even want *years* of experience doing the same things we're doing now for entry-level positions, ensuring their indoctrination is complete and that they will not have any diverse thinking.

This phenomenon seems particularly strong around how we talk about people who want to enter our industry from other industries:

We consider that some of the skills these people might have had are "transferable" to our industry, that those skills will eventually allow them to work *like us*.

Rarely if ever do I see practitioners and hiring managers look at these people and realise they have business skills, communication skills, experience in mature practices from other more mature industries. And that's before I mention objectivity, which trumps all of the above. The very things that make them diverse from hardened security practitioners. The very things that possibly makes them able to achieve better outcomes than we can.

No, instead we instead see these different skills as useless. We don't even acknowledge them, or perhaps only as, somehow, being a negative.

And that is why I have such an issue with the current push for standardisation in our industry. I see calls to define roles, what they should do, what qualifications they should hold, what a security function should look like, how operations should be structured, and much more.

But the above point with regards to "diversity" perfectly illustrates why I think this is a terrible idea.

We are not a mature industry. The trends show we are not reducing the numbers of incidents, certainly not in line with the costs to the business of doing so. And that cost to businesses is often unsustainable (consuming an ever-increasing portion of IT and company budgets).

In any case, the current approach is not effective. It doesn't stack up against proven approaches used in other industries (more on that later).

That is not something we should be standardising. It's something we should be opening to radical change.

We'll get into this a little later, but if we're to solve our problems sustainably, we're likely going to need very different skillsets.

I don't believe we currently have the workforce or skillsets we need. In fact, we often actively discriminate against the ones we do.

There will still be relevance for the roles of today, but they will have to adopt strategic, business-focused, and problem-solving mindsets rather than the current technical firefighting ones to be truly effective, and the proportions of those roles will be vastly different as we'll have far fewer fires as a result.

The Bogus Skills Gap

The "Cyber Security Skills Gap" is one of the biggest topics in cyber security. Featuring in a significant percentage of industry blogs, articles, talks, panels, and general chatter.

I'll be succinct: I think it's complete rubbish.

In my last book I made an analogy about the security industry by representing it as a car factory flinging its finished product from the third floor. It illustrated not just the lunacy of our current approach, but how it created a workforce that had the wrong skill profiles to work with the business to pre-empt problems. Worse still, as mentioned in the previous chapter, it excludes the very people and skills needed for a more sustainable approach.

I'll repeat the analogy here because it addresses what I think is a massive issue in the industry:

Imagine you're standing on the sidewalk looking at a car factory.

To one side is a huge parking lot, a staging ground for the finished cars to be shipped off for sale. On the other, the factory building itself.

Parts and sheet metal get delivered to an assembly line in the building. The metal is stamped into bodies and painted. Engines, transmissions, suspension assemblies bolted into the bodies, interiors put together and screwed into place. A complex combination of tasks over a hundred or more steps resulting in a final finished product which is then pushed out of the factory building into the parking lot.

Slight issue: We're pushing them out from the third floor.

The finished cars drop 25 feet into the lot, damaged, crumpled, and full of issues.

People rush towards them, flip them back onto their wheels, cart them to a corner of the lot, build a make-shift workspace around them, assess the damage, figure out which parts need replacing, in what order things must be disassembled and reassembled to get to them, what tools will we need for that, how do we prioritise which issues to work on first as there are so many, what is the minimum level of repair before we can send the cars off, how do we do the logistics of ordering the parts, getting the necessary tools, etc.

The crumpled cars keep coming too, every few minutes another falls from the third floor of the factory.

We're dealing with an industrial scale problem now, so we hire more people, then upgrade the tooling to work faster, buy a forklift so we can flip them and carry them off to workstations more easily.

We set up better workshops so we can work at all hours and in the rain, we start doing triage to break the issues down into different categories, new sub-disciplines are created to address specific issues faster: side damage, front end damage, drivetrain damage, electrical, upholstery, etc.

We start allocating and coordinating these workshops and more specialised teams for each to speed things up, we establish project management practices around the more complex jobs, set up workflows for cars that need multiple stations, hire more specialists and more managers to do and oversee all this work, we create management systems and quality frameworks, bring in vendors to sell us better tools and solutions, consultants to help with better methodologies for our repairs, auditors to make sure we meet our minimum standards, and so on.

Despite all this we must queue and prioritise, start implementing risk management practices to determine what's most important and what defects can we actually (hopefully) get away with because we simply can't do it all.

Maybe we'd even set up a bunch of conferences to talk about how we're doing. While we're at it, let's hand out some awards from time to time.

Because, why not? I mean we've been burning ourselves out to build and run this amazing huge multi-billion-dollar ecosystem to get these cars sorted out.

Sure, we occasionally send one out that has a massive crash due to a defect we didn't spot or address, but some of them even turn out alright!

I sometimes tell this analogy at security events and the audience starts laughing.

Because it's absurd.

And because they recognise it's them.

It's their whole industry. (Ok, a big part of it.)

We have structured a workforce of millions of people to address a problem in, at a macro level anyway, possibly the most ridiculous and inefficient way possible.

It's full of techies, and we create problems and solutions that need techies. But our problem isn't technical.

I constantly hear about this massive challenge that is the "cybersecurity skills gap," and yet every day I see people trying to "break into" the industry talking about how hard it is to get through the door.

Most of them are told they're not technical enough, or don't have enough technical experience.

The worst off are the non-technical ones. People transitioning from careers that had little to nothing to do with technology.

They're my favourites. I hire them all the time. In fact, they outnumber the technical people three to one when I build security teams.

They're the ones that haven't been indoctrinated by the security industry, they're the ones that don't automatically default to tech as the answer.

The irony is that they often stand there, intimidated by all these techies, aspiring to be them. Intimidated because they can barely grasp what's going on in our figurative parking lot and can only imagine how long and difficult the journey must be to become like them. To understand all that complexity.

I don't take them on this journey. Instead, I let them stand there for a while until they eventually swallow their pride and, embarrassed, ask me a stupid question:

"Why are we dropping the cars from the 3rd floor?"

I then have to sit them down to answer because... "You're not going to believe me, but most of these people don't see that as the problem."

"You're joking, right?"

"Sadly, I'm not. The handful that even see it, or that I hear complaining about it, don't seem able or willing to go in there and have a conversation about changing the business process to make the cars come out on the ground floor."

"Quite frankly, I think they like having the work, the importance, and they *geek out* on it."

"Would you mind walking into the factory and having a chat with them to see what we can do?"

And bam. An "unqualified" person just massively reduced our issues. More than an army of veteran tech-myopic techies ever could.

You think I'm being ridiculous? Go to your favourite job board and search for cyber or information security roles.

How many analysts, engineers, pen testers, solution consultants and other similar technical roles do you see?

Now find me a role whose job description is to identify the source of the security issues and go fix the business processes causing them. Or to go through business (including IT) processes and figure out what their security risks are. I don't know what you'd search for because as far as I can tell these roles doesn't even exist in the industry.

But I've found that most people who are a little rounded, have some common sense, some inclination for critical thinking, and half decent communication skills can quickly become pretty darn good at it.

They're also plentiful because so few people in our industry want them.

So, while we talk about a cybersecurity skills gap, I'd argue we could likely send half the security workforce home within a few years. We just have to want to fix the problem.

They'd then only need to fix the busted cars already in the parking lot, to catch up on the backlog. After that, the new cars will be rolling out on the ground floor, intact, with none or a fraction of the issues.

We need to rethink the skills we need in cybersecurity. The people I believe we need are out there, in abundance.

The only real gap, as far as I can fathom, is in leadership. Security leaders, CISOs, whatever you want to call them, that can lead people, understand business, communicate, influence, see the big picture, devise and implement strategy, and so on.

Too few of the people in charge of protecting organisations do not understand them. Many don't even communicate with them.

Even fewer can mentor, motivate, and empower teams to do so.

The logical next question is, if they could, what would they have them do?

Disconnected Strategies

In my role at CDW, I'm often presented with customers' security "strategy" documents. The ask being whether we can supply the capabilities, tools, and services the customer needs to deliver on those "strategies".

You can likely already guess why I'm using quotes.

They tend to be full of talk about generic "threats" that seem to have come from some security vendor's FUD-laden marketing material, and heaps of acronyms for technologies and capabilities around detecting, responding, and recovering from attacks.

Between the lines however, there are hints that the security function likely wouldn't know how to properly use, let alone effectively leverage, the tools and technical capabilities they are asking for. There doesn't seem to be rhyme or reason to why certain things have been selected, no mentioned to how they will be structured, integrated, operated, managed, findings actioned, etc.

They don't seem to know exactly what they are actually trying to achieve (beyond "do security") for the business, which is probably a question you should have answered before even thinking of what you need.

That brings me to the most important point: most of these strategies don't have any of connection to the organisation they are supposed to protect.

What are the specific concerns of the business? What are its revenue streams? What assets or systems are particularly critical? (Are you a bank? Are you a hospital? I expect different concerns!) Do you have challenges with legacy? What about IoT? OT? What types of vulnerabilities do you have? Why do you have them? What's causing that? What are you planning on doing to address that? What is your risk tolerance? What's the company culture like? What organisational challenges do you see facing when you will start implementing your programme? What team have you built, or will you be able to build to execute?

These are just some of dozens of questions that must be answered to formulate even the most basic of security strategies, and only at the most simplistic level.

And yet they are missing.

It's then my job to go and tell them, politely, that their security "strategy" is terrible. (Alternative words are available.)

It might surprise some that, when had at a senior management level, these conversations tend to go quite well. Clients appreciate the points on why these "strategies" would ultimately be ineffective and what is needed instead to deliver the desired outcomes.

It makes them feel like they're found good advisors, ones that make a lot of sense, and that they're in good hands. And that's good for business for us too.

However, when I must have these same discussions with "security leaders", the outcomes are often different. There is a higher likelihood of emotional resistance which can lead to things going badly. It's sometimes easier for us just to let them buy whatever they want without the advice and without the outcomes.

This because it's not unheard of for "security leaders" to stop doing business with vendors and resellers for having dared to point out flaws in their strategy.

And that bring us full circle to the beginning of this part of the book.

Many companies are stuck with bad security strategies that don't generate value, run by security functions at times too toxic to accept guidance or learn more about their organisation. Functions in turn protected by a lack of accountability due to a veil of perceived complexity, a lack of engagement, and communication skills often so poor others don't want to engage with them.

The above paragraph is harsh. In fact, it's likely the harshest paragraph of this book. I must admit I've worried on more than one occasion while writing this book that I am being too harsh on this topic. I've even discussed these concerns with several respected peers while writing as I know there are some great security functions out there.

Their feedback from these peers has been unequivocal.

"It isn't."

"No. I deal with this all the time."

"Get it out there."

"People need to hear this stuff."

Conclusion: Things are bad in a lot of places.

Now let's try to make them better.

Part Three – A Different Approach

That's enough of me ranting about the status quo and the many issues in our industry.

I now want to propose an approach that, in my experience anyway, actually works.

What if I said to you that information security shouldn't fundamentally be a risk function?

Let me rephrase that: I propose that if we want to increase the inherent security and/or resilience of our organisations, if we want to reduce risk, then risk itself isn't what we should be focusing on.

We should be focusing on what, at the most fundamental level, causes the risks to exist in the first place.

I'd touched on this in *Rethinking InfoSec*, but only in the last two or three years has a very simple concept emerged in my mind that sums it all up.

It turns out I was about 30 years behind the curve as this concept is widely accepted and effective in many industries and I've met a few security outsiders who couldn't understand why we didn't use it either.

That concept is *quality*. What if we should be a quality function instead?

Why Quality Is Better

What do I mean by quality?

Let me see if I can quickly make that relatable for you by going back to my earlier car factory analogy.

In it I explained a scenario where finished cars were damaged by being dropped from the third floor and a whole firefighting ecosystem was born to mitigate and fix all the damage that was suffered.

This analogy is, of course, silly. The reason I tell it that way is that it makes the concept easier to grasp (it's a faster delivery) and adds some dramatic effect.

A more realistic analogy would be one where the cars are not getting damaged from being dropped at the end, but rather accumulating incremental defects through issues in process or consistency at one or more of the stations making up the assembly line.

The result is still the same: a never-ending number of cars coming off the line with defects that need sorting.

In most other industries, as soon as we had one or, at most, a handful of defects of a certain type or class, we would work out why it was happening on the line and sort it there.

Having to deal with damage at the end, even just sending things back to be fixed, is a rarity to be avoided. And yet, somehow, in security it's our modus operandi.

Note that I said "types" or "classes" of issues. What I mean by this is that a loose brake calliper, suspension arm, steering column, transmission mount, could all be related to the same process(es) we use to ensure bolts are tightly fastened.

If we detect this problem first time due to a loose brake calliper, that doesn't make it a brake calliper problem. And addressing the underlying problem of bolts loosening, like using more accurate torque wrenches or preventing torque settings from being accidentally changed, or use some Loctite (other brands are available), will result in all the other bolt loosening issues (whether they relate to poorly secured suspension arms, transmission mounts, or wheel lugs.) to never happen in the first place, even if we never detected them or anticipated them.

This is a crucial element of quality management, it means we can prevent much more, more than we even know about, and that gains (in quality or the reduction of defects) are not only asymmetrical, but also *cumulative*.

In other words, you would not typically need to fix the same issue more than once, and fixing one issue can solve multiple problems.

In my mind, it's why the trends around the number of defects (in construction, configuration, design, architecture, process, human behaviour, etc.) and their associated incidents in industries that apply common sense quality management approaches look like this:

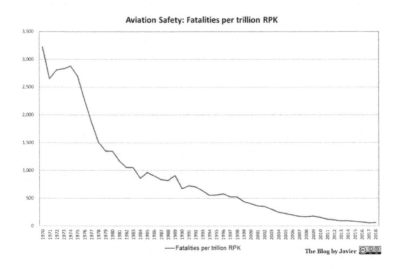

While in security [despite increasing spending], due to the lack of a holistic (beyond the "security" silo) quality management approach, the trends look like this:

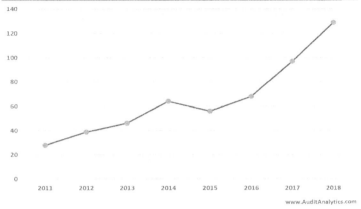

www.AuditAnalytics.com

Feel free to replace this chart with any of the thousands of others online showing a similar trend (as in, pretty much all of them).

And that's as good as an introduction as I can give on why, at least in the long run, quality matters a whole lot more than chasing individual risks like we tend to do today.

Manufacturing industries have a handful of quality assurance people at the end of the build process that detect defects and work out how they were caused and how to prevent them.

In security we instead hire millions of people and spend billions in tooling to try and mitigate risks presented by those defects. Why?

Defects & Benefits

Let's firm up the relationship between quality and security, and why looking at it this way is so advantageous not just for security, but for business.

One big fringe benefit off the quality approach is that it's so easy to explain to anyone. In fact, the more removed they are from all the preconceptions about "security" the more they get it.

I like to ask executives "What is security?"

Or rather, why are breaches happening?

My answer: Vulnerabilities. Attackers exploit vulnerabilities.

But what is a vulnerability? How about *a defect*?

A defect in code, in a system, in a build, in architecture, in a configuration, in a process, or even in human behaviour.

A defect in any of those things that allows something to be made to do something that it shouldn't be doing. Whether that be execute something, overwrite something, provide access to something, anything.

But are those *security* defects?

What if, instead, we thought of them as *quality* defects?

Because the causes behind any defect that allows something unintentional to happen are likely the same whether that defect has a security repercussion or not.

For example, an error in some code that causes an application to be unstable, or one that inadvertently hands an attacker administrative permission, are both caused by poor programming practices. Arguably only one is a security concern from a breach point of view, but they share a root cause.

By improving *quality*, of programming practices in this case, we not only reduce the amount of security issues we are likely to see produced, but also improve the stability of the application. If this application is internal, that means higher productivity, if it's a product we sell, that means happier customers, fewer complaints, less rework, and a reduction in all the associated costs.

Suddenly, security is not only addressing root causes and driving sustainable decreases in security issues, it's also generating cost efficiencies and productivity gains outside the security department as they suffered from the same root causes.

Some examples of quality defects picked up by security functions I've ran include identifying software architecture issues, failures by HR to automate workflows, poor engineering practices, bad (expensive) licensing models, and excessive resource consumption.

In one case, chasing why we were seeing vulnerable assets provisioned a certain way, we identified excess AWS usage in the hundreds of thousands of Euros per month.

In another, not understanding why things were being tested in a certain way, we discovered fundamental architectural failures that identified knowledge, skill, and experience deficiencies in development teams.

In yet one more, trying to reduce the number of administrative users on a CRM platform a department had self-provisioned, we were able to restructure the functional workflow as to reduce license costs by nearly €50,000 per year. (We hired an outside firm to perform this work with a one-time cost of €23,000.)

We increased the business's bottom line by addressing problems through quality improvements rather than "risk management".

We found similar cost efficiencies almost everywhere we looked. And we looked there because we determined those areas as the sources of security issues, *due to quality issues*. These quality issues weren't just introducing unnecessary risk, they were introducing unnecessary costs.

Perhaps the most remarkable case was us tracing quality issues in how our infrastructure was built to the turnover of good DevOps and Site Reliability Engineers, whose absence and replacement delays were impacting product delivery timelines and incurring significant recruiting costs and effort. The poor quality of the platforms they had to maintain was resulting in them burning out and leaving. It was also causing security issues, which is how we got involved as worked our way back to their root causes.

We'll go deeper on why a quality management approach works better from a security standpoint in a moment. The point I'm trying to make here specifically is that a quality approach has many *business* benefits well beyond reducing the risk of security incidents.

This opens up conversations and interest at the senior-most levels of the organisations.

I hear many security practitioners lament that senior management teams don't care about risk.

I'd argue that they do, but they care about *business* risk.

As far as them not caring about cyber risk, yeah, that's possibly true. Does it matter? Probably not.

Like most things in business, security should be a bottom-line proposition. That's something many security functions I've come across haven't been able to articulate, and I'm not surprised because I'm not sure the proposition is even there to be made with the current status quo approach and results.

By contrast, switching to a business-focused quality management approach means we start creating real tangible and measurable *financial benefit* to the organisation. That is something we can get traction and support on at the senior-most levels.

The risk reduction is just a by-product. We don't even necessarily need to quantify it, especially if we can generate positive ROI just on the business benefits of quality.

Knowing the business impact to the bottom line, as to prioritise the greatest benefit first, is obviously still a good idea. I'm just saying we can potentially still be a net positive to the business either way.

We can reduce risk in a way that's more sustainable over time, while directly helping the bottom line, which gets us the trust and support from senior leadership to also do the [necessary] things that may be less tangible.

The Pitch

One of the hardest parts of my job at CDW is reaching the right people to help organisations with their security strategies.

It may surprise you, although maybe less so after reading the first part of this book, that it's often not the "security people", in which I unfortunately include many CISOs.

They usually want to buy tools and tech, and quite often either don't understand or are put off by conversations tying in business process and quality-based improvements.

The audiences I'm looking for tend to be CIO and up as they care more about business outcomes and less about technology for technology's sake. They are also more likely to have the needed influence to successfully implement a holistic (and therefore effective) security strategy. (Which we can then sell to.)

Unfortunately, this audience often assumes I'm going to be one of those "security people" and they don't want to talk to me as a result.

(Yet another example of how bad the perception we have created for ourselves in security is, and how it holds us back.)

To get the meetings with my needed audience, and to hold their attention before I'm dismissed, I've had to come up with several quick analogies.

I want to share one with you which we'll refer back to throughout the book.

Imagine your company builds passenger planes.

At some point you realise that the bolts that secure the wings on your planes slacken during flight, which will eventually result in a catastrophic disaster.

Needless to say, this will be extraordinarily bad for business.

So, you build workshops in every airport in the world and staff them with engineers and specialist equipment to continuously inspect and tighten the bolts after every flight to minimise the risk of the dreaded catastrophic incident happening.

The first time I ran this analogy past a colleague (who does not work in security) I'd barely gotten to "you build workshops in every airport..." when he immediately interrupted me with "No you wouldn't! That's *stupid*!"

Exactly.

What you would do is work closely with all relevant parts of the business, including senior management, to immediately have the design changed so that this wasn't an issue anymore (and then use what was learned in every future design). You'd then retrofit or retire what was out there, and the issue would be solved, for good.

The latter solution just makes a lot more sense, from a risk reduction standpoint, a risk reduction *over time* standpoint, and a business operational cost standpoint.

This isn't even worth explaining to senior business leaders, it's a given. I'm only saying it here to give context to the pitch.

I then ask them why most security is done like the former rather than the latter?

During the almost inevitable pause I like to throw in the mice and grain analogy I mentioned before.

"Do I have a mouse problem or a grain storage problem?"

That usually gives me time to run the spiel about what security is. Vulnerabilities being exploited. What causes them? Quality issues/defects, how do we reduce those? Look at the results in other industries.

At this point I'm no longer in the "security person" category. They're interested, they're curious, they see the potential for benefit in their own organisations, and they're open (sometimes even eager) to discuss things further or make the right introductions.

The plane pitch has some shock value, it's a different and disruptive take on security they've not heard before. The mice and quality arguments are less shocking but possibly even more different and thought provoking.

And yet they are the opposite of what disruptive arguments usually are: immediately logical, easy to understand, obvious, and relatable.

It means they become interested. Better still, they are now part of the conversation. There's nothing technical about it, it's logical, they get it.

They also usually *see* it.

They rapidly realise this is their organisation too, and that things could be done better, that so many of the logical things they do to optimise things apply to security outcomes as well.

That [their] common sense is possibly superior at solving security challenges than all the special technical knowledge security professionals covet, is, a bit of a vindication too (as well as a little ego boost).

To summarise: This is no longer a technical conversation. And that's what makes it accessible, even exciting, to the C-levels. More importantly, it makes it *relevant* to them.

It makes them want to have that discussion.

Scalability

I want to run some simple but very important math by you, because it shows us something important:

Not only does our current approach mean we have to keep scaling security to keep up with the risks [of ever-increasing threats taking advantage of ever-increasing vulnerabilities], but even with 1:1 scaling of security resource to the business, the risk of a major incident still increases linearly with the size of the business.

Let me try to make that clearer by going back to our plane example.

We have 200 planes in service. Each makes 500 flights per year. That's 100,000 flights per year.

By inspecting and retightening the wing bolts we reduce the odds of disaster (a wing coming off) on any given flight to one in a million, or 0.0001%.

In other words, we have an average chance of this disaster happening once for every million flights.

We have 100,000 flights per year, 1/10th of one million.

I.e.: There is a 10% chance of this disaster happening in a given year.

We take that risk.

Business is good, we keep growing and producing, as such we deliver another 400 planes.

There are now 600 total, three times as many as the 200 there were last year.

They're each flying the same 500 flights per year each.

Logically, that means we have three times as many flights per year. 600 planes x 500 flights each = 300,000.

Now, since we have three times the fleet, we have also tripled the size of the bolt tightening operation. Three times the workspace, three times the staff, three times the tools, three times the cost to the business.

As a result, we are able to maintain the same 0.0001% risk of disaster per flight across the fleet.

But we have three times more flights.

The probability of a disaster within the year isn't 10% anymore. It's 30%.

Those are worrisome odds. And they're going to get worse the more the business grows, despite increasing the spending accordingly.

Some security practitioners might argue that the business is bigger so it should absorb more incidents, but I'd like to see them get their leadership teams and their customers to agree (for an array of financial and reputational reasons).

In any case, if we, like almost every other industry, used a quality management approach instead, not only would the risk of a particular incident occurring decrease over time, but the business' infrastructure increasing in size would not significantly contribute towards an increase in the frequency of the risk occurring, because the fundamental issue (root cause) that could lead to it has been addressed.

In other words: a quality management approach means we don't allow the problems to exist, let alone scale.

As opposed to our current approach which doesn't focus on stopping issues from scaling, instead scaling up capacity to respond to the increasing scale of the problems.

This is simply not sustainable, and the trends both in terms of spending and incidents back this up.

Quality Management and Security Tools

I used to be a massive techie. Security tools were cool, I loved tools. I was always making up whatever argument to get the latest and coolest tools. Yes, I was one of those "security people".

It was not exactly mature of me. I then got older and started having a more holistic, business-focused, and process driven view. I think I just started caring more about the problem, the business, and the people.

What was the point of having the world's fanciest "Next Generation" "AI-powered" (other buzzwords are available) tool to detect attacks when I had no architectural standards, no idea what my assets were, didn't know what permissions my users needed to do what, hadn't patched my applications in years, etc?

People that do this care more about playing with cool toys than protecting the business' bottom line, and usually fail to do so. I was that guy, and I reached a point where I wanted to be anything but that guy.

This "anti-tool" opinion was quite strong in *Rethinking InfoSec*, which was published over three years ago (with some of its material older than that). I advocated that the drive for new security tools be paused, and that people start focusing on the basics instead. The kind of stuff I mentioned in the "Burning Money" chapter earlier in this book.

But my thinking has now matured some more and so it may surprise some returning readers that my position on the importance of tooling has changed.

You see, I realised that my objection isn't so much with the tools as it is with how we use them. Or, rather, how we *don't* use them.

What we've learned through decades of maturing quality management approaches is that it makes a lot more sense to fix problems at source (in our car assembly analogy: the station where the problem is being introduced - and potentially further up still) than at the end of the line (hiring a hoard of bodies to manage and remedy the never-ending stream of defects).

So where does tooling fit in?

Let's look at vulnerability management as an example.

Your typical solution will use a combination of APIs, agents, or scanning engines to detect vulnerabilities on systems and then present you the findings.

The interfaces of such tools have become increasingly clever; sorting the vulnerabilities by type, by criticality score, by complexity to exploit, by which are on internet-facing systems thereby increasing the likelihood of exploitation, which have known published exploit code, which are actively being exploited in the wild right now, etc.

All of these things allow you to approach remediation more strategically, more effectively.

By which I mean the tool will show me that, say, 3,000 new vulnerabilities have appeared in my environment this year and allow me to prioritise which ones need to be fixed first thanks to all the additional context about criticality, exploitability, exposure, etc.

Except, if we broaden the scope, that's not really strategic at all.

In our car assembly line analogy, it's the equivalent of helping the people in the parking lot prioritise what on the damaged cars should be repaired first.

As a strategic CISO with a long-term goal of reducing risk and cost to the organisation I don't really care about this.

Instead, I look at the vulnerabilities and ask myself *what's causing them.* I want to stop the cars from having defects in the first place.

If we have thousands of missing patches, then my strategic priority isn't to have tickets opened to patch all of these systems. It's to implement a working patching process (or find out why our existing one isn't working).

If we have poor configurations enabling insecure services then I want to look into, or establish, configuration standards and management.

If we have vulnerabilities due to poor in house coding and engineering practices, I'm going to go do what it takes to address that.

If I see our hostnames are all over the place, or that people can't identify systems we've found, I'm going to go sort our asset management and maybe our procurement processes.

My job is to talk to anyone, C-level on down, whose area may have a role in these issues and help them to change those IT/business processes to improve their outputs.

By addressing a handful of such issues, you can often stop the continued generation of a significant portion of the problems that keep security teams busy around the clock.

By doing this, next year I won't have 3,000 vulnerabilities, I'll have maybe 800, I can then look into their root causes and have a lower number still the following year, and so on.

That is a strategic approach to fixing the problem long-term. As opposed to merely prioritising the work resulting from the failure to fix the real issue.

In the context of our plane analogy, we've now fixed the design issue. Every new plane leaving the line will no longer have this issue. We only need to fix or retire what's already in the field, *once*. Better yet, the lessons learned will mean even fewer issues in the future when we build the next model plane.

Security teams burn themselves out trying to meet SLAs on how quickly they remediate a never-ending stream of new vulnerabilities when they should be fixing the business and IT issues causing them. Our SLAs should be around by how much we reduce issues, not how many issues we handle.

We don't do this. Our tools aren't designed for this. But it doesn't mean they can't be used for it.

We need to start thinking about how we can unlock their strategic value.

Incidentally, this has been a big part of my work with vendors over the past year: coming up with strategic uses that allowed customers to reap much higher value from tools than what the vendor initially intended.

(There are some prime examples of this in the Hitachi Vantara blog series included at the end of this book, where we look at how storage and recovery can support and enable a more strategic approach to security.)

Quality & Hit Rate

I want to take a moment to discuss something that is not specifically related to the previous chapter (strategic use of tools) but often enabled by it.

A few years ago, before I'd truly woken up to the whole security as quality thing (but doing elements of it without realising), I wrote an article for an automated penetration testing vendor.

As always, I tried to create a narrative where we get more strategic value out of tools.

What I came up with aligns rather well to the quality proposition, illustrating yet one more benefit of it:

It's not just better to go after root causes rather than fighting every resulting technical issue, it's a lot easier to identify them too. Because fighting symptoms requires us to find every symptom in order to be effective, there are dozens, hundreds, or thousands of symptoms for each root cause. That means we can miss *loads* and still accurately find most of our root causes.

What I focused on in that article was that one of the main criticisms or questions about automated penetration testing is whether it's as good as manual human testing.

Let's ignore the fact that this depends largely on the skill of the human tester (which raises some points about consistency) and state that a good human tester always has a higher *potential* of finding something. A human will have more creativity, flexibility, and anything automated has to be built which means it's potentially behind the curve. It's built by a human so it *can't* be smarter.

However, with the quality approach, this *does not matter.*

There is no need for me to find every vulnerability because, at a strategic level, I don't care about each and every vulnerability.

My goal is to find and address root causes, and each root cause will likely manifest many symptoms, or issues, or vulnerabilities. Which means I will have multiple opportunities to find a thread to pull on to lead me to that one root cause.

In other words, I only need to find *one* vulnerability per root cause to track it down and deal with it. Which means, if done properly, I'll have prevented virtually every instance of that type.

Back to the plane analogy with the bolts holding the wings slackening during flight: Not every bolt needed to be loose to see that there was a problem, one out of hundreds would have been enough. And solving that problem with a bolt or fastener design that doesn't allow slackening will not just prevent the issue with the wings, but any future bolt slackening issue in any other part of the plane where I use the new design to fasten something.

To give an example from IT-land, imagine I have several issues in my in-house applications that allow privilege escalation.

Some are simple and can be found by the most basic of security scanners. Others may be significantly harder to detect, to the point that only the most skilled human tester with a large amount of time would pick it up.

But they are caused by the same issue, the same behaviour, the same coding practices, the same root cause.

Applying a quality management approach means any finding can help us prevent a whole class of issues in the future, we do not need to find all of them. And that, once again, is how we get a cumulative decrease of issues over time.

Another benefit of only needing to find one indicator of each root cause is that we save a tremendous amount of effort that can be reallocated elsewhere.

In the case of an automated penetration solution (although this approach applies to anything) we have the advantage of *scope*. I can look, perhaps less meticulously (only enough to find one symptom of each root cause to go attack), but in more areas.

Different areas with different business processes, types of platforms, teams, and working cultures are far more likely to have different root causes to their issues. That's why, strategically, breadth of findings is more important than exhaustive technical depth. You might not find every vulnerability, but you will find more root causes. That's far more important in terms of reducing new issues/sources of vulnerabilities over time, freeing up resource to sort your backlog, and only needing to do it once.

There's even the extreme scenario of not remediating anything, because eventually it will all get replaced anyway, and by that time you'll hopefully have defined what good looks like for anything coming down the pipe.

This is not to say that you shouldn't fix critical issues you currently have in your environment, but that we should focus as much resource to addressing root causes as that's the only way we'll eventually solve the core problem.

It's like bailing water out of a sinking boat without ever trying to stop the leaks letting that water in. The sooner you stop the leaks, the less water you will have to bail overall, even if it means taking on a bit more water in the short term. That is a risk and cost proposition that the business should balance.

In closing, I think you'll find that, once explained, a focus on the strategic [quality-driven] approach and its many additional business benefits is what most sensible senior management teams want from their CISOs.

Even if it means those executives accepting a higher level of risk on the short term.

Quality And The CISO

In my opinion, a huge part of the stress that I see CISOs complain about comes from the lack of a pragmatic, strategic, long-term approach to doing security.

That's a lot of fancy words but I am referring simply to the fact that most CISOs spend their time trying to build up operational security capacity to deal with a never-ending and ever-increasing number of risks and vulnerabilities.

This instead of acting *truly* strategically to reduce the number of issues they would need to deal with over time (and their cost to the business) by influencing the quality of the organisation's IT and business process outputs.

We've talked about the former approach being unsustainable as it requires functions to endlessly scale, in turn introducing evermore complexity, and create more to manage and more room for error. This inevitably boosts the probability of a breach.

But at a human level it's equally unsustainable for a CISO to manage that kind of never-ending workload which only keeps increasing in scale and breadth.

Even just from a purely psychological standpoint, there is simply no satisfaction in firefighting a problem that is only getting worse, requiring more and more time and headspace, with no hope of progress. It's a recipe for burnout. And not just for CISOs either.

Conversely, if a CISO works on changing the business process and, as a result, sees the business generating fewer and fewer issues over time, that is tangible and there is psychological reward.

It's far more likely a CISO will stay motivated and push forward with that kind of approach where continuous progress is being made. That CISO will likely want to keep driving that progress, leaving only once the task is accomplished and the operational security work required to keep the company safe has been brought down to a low and easily sustainable level.

This as opposed to the trend I often see of CISOs burning out in 18 months and starting over somewhere else.

Interesting aside here: It seems noteworthy to me how often new CISOs come in and radically change the security "strategy", tooling, team structures, and more. Essentially changing how firefighting will be done, but not reducing the amount of firefighting needed. That's especially interesting as the business (and its needs) won't have changed much between those CISOs. Another hint at the disconnect between the business reality and how many security functions operate.

Back to the upsides for the CISO... There is no doubt in my mind that influencing the business to reduce the number of defects produced for security to "deal with" is a far more effective use of a CISO's time.

I suspect some readers are now thinking that all sounds great, but the reality is the CISO doesn't have the support from senior management to make those business changes.

To this my argument (and the one of a handful of other CISOs I've come across) is that you, as a CISO are responsible for creating those conditions for yourself.

Either don't accept a role where you don't have the authority or influence the management to put you in that position. No one is saying it's easy, but that's the role of a good CISO.

To that aim, I'm hoping this book provides some ideas and arguments that can help you in achieving that in the same way they've helped me.

Just by itself, quality management approach has some selling points that can really help us get some traction to that end.

Firstly, it's a *lot* easier to communicate to an executive audience. I've yet to come across an executive that didn't understand it (unlike all the usual sea of security technologies, acronyms, frameworks, etc. they're usually told) and see the potential for significant advantages.

Secondly, once they understand the premise, you won't be expected to fight fires nearly as much as it's very clear to them that the strategic work you are doing is more important, or rather *of greater business benefit*, than the technical or operational work that they might have originally expected of a CISO.

As a result, it behoves the business to free you of such responsibilities. That's the job of a Head of Information Security [Operations] or similar title who should report to you (or elsewhere) to handle the operational security side of the house.

This frees you of a lot of stress, not to mention the accountability for pre-existing issues, and issues produced by other departments.

Which brings us to the third point: it destroys the argument that other departments aren't responsible for their own security.

How? By no longer calling it security.

The security industry has created and reinforced the notion that it is a terribly complex field that should be left to elite and highly paid professionals because you couldn't possibly understand all the incredible amazing stuff they do to save the world every day.

And by "reinforcing" I mean screaming it from the rooftops ad nauseum.

And thus, we now have a strong perception that security is a specialist activity that should be done by specialists and not mere mortals.

It's therefore no surprise that when you tell an executive that the Engineering, or Sales, or whatever department's outputs have security issues that they need to resolve rather than pushing them onto the business (and onto your security team), the reaction is usually "Well? Their job is Engineering, Sales, or whatever. Security is *your* job. Isn't it? What do we pay you for?"

But what if we called it quality instead?

We expect the people building something to be responsible, and accountable, for its quality.

Most industries do not set up completely separate departments to fix defects from their other functions. They expect the quality of a department's output to be the responsibility of that department.

A quality assurance function in that context is mostly there as validation and to instruct other departments on what they need to improve, not mitigate the consequences of their poor quality.

When I get objections to this from departments insisting security is a specialised thing and *not* their responsibility, I like asking them which specialist locked their front door this morning. But ultimately, I find the leadership team would rather get them to sort the issues with their outputs than give me a few extra million per year to mitigate them.

Bringing accountability to other parts of the business may mean I get less budget and a smaller team, but it's also a measure of my contribution to the business.

Delivering results rather than costs gets me appreciated where it matters and empowers me personally to get the job done.

On that note, I want to advise companies to stop hiring CISOs based on the headcount and budgets of their predecessors. These are just as likely to be a sign of bloat and inefficacy as they are of competence. Especially if they kept growing without an appreciable and measurable decrease in issues and incidents.

And by "incidents" I mean the number the security team tackled, not that the business felt. Many security functions show how many millions of incidents they handled in a year as proof of the important work they are doing but in some ways it could be argued that's actually a sign that the fundamental security of the organisation is bad and isn't being improved.

And that is a recipe of breaches *and* Burnout. It's not fair to the business, or the CISO.

Quality as an Indicator

I used to do freelance work where my job was to show negligence in security functions so that insurers wouldn't have to pay out after a breach.

Doing so meant demonstrating such a failure in due care that it would be irrefutable that there was negligence that would inevitably lead to a breach, and it had to be so obvious that it could easily be argued and understood in court to a judge or jury should the company challenge the finding.

I had a 100% success rate, and it never took very long.

It came down to asking the same questions about quality we've already covered. Why they'd never addressed the sources of the thousands of new security vulnerabilities the business added every year, why there wasn't even a plan to do so, whether the senior management had visibility or understanding of security activities, whether security reviewed how business processes operated or were even planning to do so, and so on.

The negligence was usually palpable, obvious to anyone that knew what to look for.

Not once did the General Counsel of one of these companies challenge our findings. Not once did things go to court. I can only imagine how surprised they were at the obviousness of what should have been done and stunned that it wasn't.

It's back to that disconnect between business and security. Neither side understanding each other.

Let me clarify that I'm not saying it's impossible to be breached when doing a good job. There is always some risk, but it's exponentially less likely to be from a class of issue you've addressed the root cause of.

My definition of negligence also considers time and direction. If a company is breached but the CISO had a well thought out [and well prioritised] plan that would have led them to *eventually* discover and remediate the issue at fault, I don't see that as negligent.

Negligence is when there is no direction, everything is operational (and at times of dubious effectiveness) without an effort to continuously improve the understanding of business, validate the scope, or try to address the root causes.

There is, unfortunately, often an element of disregard or dereliction of duty involved as well; security functions coasting due to the lack of visibility and accountability of their actions.

I do not have enough fingers to count the number of times I've heard of a company having a breach, a new CIO being brought in, and the Head of Information Security or CISO quickly resigning (or being sacked) afterwards as the new CIO looks into things and finds that the security "leadership" had been doing very little indeed.

Some of these security leaders were burning their time on work of little strategic or tangible benefit, which could be considered a lack of competence, but some actively hid behind that wall created by the perceived complexity of "security" and their own poor communication skills which kept people at bay.

Now think about an organisation that ran its security as a quality management function as described over the last several chapters. Would such situations occur there?

I don't think they would. It's too visible, the benefits too measurable, the interactions too wide, its position too close to senior management, and as a result it's too accountable to get away with this kind of negligence, let alone malfeasance.

I've noticed that one of the manifestations of truly mature organisations (with regards to security) is a high level of business process maturity rather than an extensive list of [at times poorly implemented] security technologies.

In fact, the organisations with the best security may even have less in terms of security tools and staff than their peers.

Firstly, because it's less likely for there to be a culture of waste. One would instead expect to find one of getting the most out of everything, delivering strategic value, and giving back to the business where possible.

Secondly, because they simply don't have the problems to warrant the extra tools and staff. They'd have fewer issues, more consistency, less unnecessary complexity to work around, and so forth.

How significant is this?

I've long had a cynical view about certifications like ISO27001. I know first-hand they're often not worth the paper they're printed on in terms of risk reduction or indicating whether an organisation is "secure" or has a reasonable level of security maturity.

In fact, they're often used to make up for the lack of said maturity. Can't be transparent about being secure? Get a certification that [sort of] says you are. Easy!

But what's been blowing my mind over the last few years is how cyber insurers, who have a direct financial liability, are still basing their due diligence and insurability assessments on these certifications.

They are taking losses on clients they should never have insured, and whose pay-outs could have been objected to on the grounds of negligence.

This got me thinking about what we should be looking at during the due diligence process. My conclusion, and what I now advise insurance companies, is to shift the focus away from "security controls" and to instead look at the quality and maturity of business and IT processes of those seeking insurance.

It makes perfect sense to me, and it made a lot of sense to non-technical insurance audiences too. I've even had some well-known reinsurers contact me about hearing me speak on the subject.

If you are flooding a siloed tech function with thousands of security issues, things are far more likely to be missed than if you have high-quality processes that only result on the odd manageable exception.

In summary, the quality of business and IT processes (which includes security considerations) is possibly a better indicator of how likely an organisation is to suffer a breach, how heavy that breach will be, and how much they will struggle to recover, than the mere presence of "security" technologies and controls.

It's also harder to tick-box away.

Quality and the Status Quo

Quality management is essentially a mindset that we should have in everything we do if we're to reduce the defects that make us vulnerable.

So far, we have been talking about that in the context of the business and IT processes themselves.

But there is another area that also suffers from a lack of quality that sits a bit closer to the status quo security functions of today. By which I mean the implementation of "security" tooling, processes, and controls.

A huge portion of security tooling today is poorly or partially implemented.

Penetration tests are poorly scoped, Vulnerability Management platforms not well configured, FW/IDS/IPS/EDR/MDR/XDR/SIEM/IAM definitions/rules/actions/response processes poorly defined, and much more.

I also want to highlight issues with dependencies in regard to security tooling. For example, an EDR agent reporting from a vulnerable and compromised host is potentially also compromised and only reporting what an attacker wants it to. Something few security teams even consider.

My point is that even with the deluge of events and incidents caused by the failure to address root causes today, the amount of security technologies in place in many organisations should still at least *detect* most attacks. In my experience they often don't.

While they have tooling that *should* be able to provide virtually real-time detection of breaches, the reality is that many are actually detecting them hundreds of days after they occur. And often due to being notified by a third party!

In my mind, building resilient processes and IT is the best defence against attacks, but we will always need *some* detection and response capability. It's therefore important to make sure we apply quality processes to those capabilities too.

Part Four – Commercialising Security

Security is typically considered a "risk function", but we've now seen that applying a quality management approach to reduce risk long-term can add many additional business benefits like reduced waste, increased efficiency, even improvements in communication and culture.

But what about generating direct commercial benefit? In other words, we've seen how it can improve the bottom line, but what about the top line?

I feel we're not just missing these potential contributions to our organisations here, but also opportunities for conversations with, and support from, our business stakeholders.

Commercial Security Strategy

I'm probably repeating myself here, but most organisations don't have what I'd consider a good security strategy. Heck, most don't even have a security strategy *at all*.

And no, implementing NIST or ISO is *not* a security strategy.

Most of the security strategies I get submitted are *terrible* with no consideration of what's important to the business, and no consideration as to what is causing their security issues, or "fragility", in the first place.

But what I haven't mentioned yet is that almost none of them have *commercial* security strategies.

In fact, I suspect few practitioners have even thought about it.

It's a simple concept. Try to think of a commercial security goal. How can security contribute to the business, not in terms of risk, but commercially.

You think about that and, once you've identified a goal, define a strategy to reach that goal.

Let me give you an example.

Last year I was approached for a CISO role with a well-known UK brand encompassing 50 or so large higher-end department stores.

Let's call them Jon Louis.

I asked what their commercial security strategy was.

The answer I got was that they had a focus on securing their Point-of-Sale devices.

This was an alarmingly specific technical task (out of many thousands, I assume) for what should have been a C-level role. It's also not a commercial strategy.

I've never worked in a brick-and-mortar retail organisation, but this is what I proposed to them remembering a story I'd heard about Target.

Forgive any inaccuracy here as I'm doing this from memory, but the general principle will be clear.

Target is a large US retail chain selling everything from food to furniture.

About 20 years ago (well before the advent of cloud and big data), they developed the ability to figure something out with a remarkable amount of accuracy: when their customers were pregnant.

Now, if you think about it, a pregnant woman is a dream demographic for Target. They drive a huge amount of new purchasing for things like baby food, diapers, care products, swings, strollers, car seats, clothes, childproofing, toys, books, decorations, maternity products, and much more.

The spend is *significant*. The revenue opportunities immense.

Here's the kicker: They often figured out when a customer was pregnant *before* they bought anything you'd normally associate with pregnancy.

In fact, they frequently worked out customers were pregnant *before the customers knew it themselves.*

There were allegedly incidents of fathers, husbands, and boyfriends outraged that their daughter, wife, or girlfriend was receiving targeted marketing fliers clearly meant for pregnant women, only to have to come back weeks later and apologise, because they were in fact pregnant.

You can only imagine how successful this was not only in getting those customers to do their initial parenthood shopping there, but to continue shopping there, and then bring their children there, every week of their lives, moulding them into future customers.

So successful indeed that there are now memes, YouTube videos, and even marketing campaigns by Target themselves about male support groups forming in the Target parking lot as their female partners and children disappear into the store for hours on end.

That is the power of targeted marketing, and targeted marketing is powered by *data*.

A quick bit of research shows Jon Louis' growth is stagnant, profits have been down, employee bonuses have disappeared, and their customer demographic is aging out.

Imagine if you had data about your customers that would allow you to target your marketing to them? To make it so that you reminded them that Jon Louis had what *they* needed.

Not just for their everyday lives, but for targeted personal events like that upcoming birthday, or that of a spouse, or child, a teenager's prom, graduation, etc.

Imagine making it a habit for them to come to your store because you are the one that responds to and reminds them of their needs.

Imagine them bringing friends and children into the store with them, creating new customers, potentially a whole new generation of them.

What do you need to achieve this?

You need people to trust you with their data. Something people are increasingly reluctant to do. Why? Poor security and the possibility of their data being compromised for one.

In this scenario at least, that could be the goal of the security function from a commercial standpoint.

That means we'd need to do security well. Not though tick-boxing or third-party compliance, and not with an IT-only focus.

We'd have to build a security programme that understands the importance of customer trust and therefore has a specific focus on it.

That means understanding where customer data comes from, where it's used, how it's commercialised, how it's processed, where it's stored, etc. By every part of the business.

We can then start talking about it, showcasing the depth of care we take with our customer's data. Demonstrate that we track every phase of the data's journey, that we are aware of the risks, all the steps we take to address those risks, etc., etc.

We can build messaging about it; we can even challenge our competitors on it.

There's even an opportunity there to lead the curve as the public becomes more aware and concerned about their data.

They must shop somewhere, so who takes better care of their data will only increase in importance. I doubt it will ever overshadow other factors like the actual products being sold and the marketing and branding around them, but it can play a role. And getting people to feel more at ease about sharing that information with our business can be a powerful, even crucial, element in empowering those other factors.

We could take it further still:

Many people pay a monthly fee to firms who monitor their credit scores and online accounts. Let's say £4.95, though I've seen double that.

What if Jon Louis did that, for free?

You've potentially just shifted the customer thought process from:

"I'm increasingly savvy and careful about my personal data so I'm not going to share it with any stores."

To:

"I'm increasingly savvy and careful about my personal data so I'm going to give it to Jon Louis so they can monitor it for me."

And that could be our commercial security strategy in this situation, to help empower the other parts of the business that lead to sales. In this case by helping push the access to information the business needs to thrive.

It could be any number of other things like security as a brand value, a competitive differentiator, a higher level of integrity and assurance than competitors for mission critical services, etc.

We should always try to protect the organisation's bottom line. We all claim to do this by reducing risk, but we also need to minimise our cost to the business. As with any cost-centre it's part of our job to be as cost efficient as possible.

By commercialising security, we add another dimension to our value. We become more than a cost-centre; we help increase the business' top line too. This obviously offsets our cost, potentially entirely, and grows the bottom line too.

Coming full circle, creating that additional value, being a business contributor, also increases our standing within the business. This in turn gives us more traction to influence business process and reduce risk.

In conclusion, by creating a security strategy that gives the business *commercial* benefits, we can significantly increase the traction of the security function to deliver on the risk proposition too.

Sometimes these activities can be quite separate, or tightly intertwined, depending on your business.

A Better Garage

Another car analogy for you, but feel free to adapt to your personal interests/addiction(s).

Let's say I own a beautiful classic car. It's my pride and joy. I worry that others don't appreciate it the way I do, and that includes garages. I simply don't trust them that much.

Every so often it needs work done, or a complicated service I can't do myself. I have no choice; I *must* take it to a garage.

Typically, that goes something like this:

I drive up, go into a reception space, they take my keys, and someone drives my car into the back somewhere out of sight, where I'm not allowed to go.

I can leave or wait in the reception area for a few hours until I'm told my car is ready. When it is, I'm handed a list of things they've done, usually in the form of a bill, that looks something like this:

1. Found X was loose, sorted it.
2. Noticed Y was worn so changed that.
3. Changed the oil and filter.
4. Etc.

The fact is, I have no idea whether this was truly done.

This is not dissimilar to your average security questionnaire, or Statement of Work.

Can I actually validate that all of this has been done?

Fun fact: I mark the oil filters on my cars before taking them into dealerships to be serviced and half the time I find the filters (and likely the oil) haven't been changed despite being stated as part of the service and a new filter appearing on my bill.

And I regret to say that in my years auditing companies' security functions, I've seen much the same.

I just don't trust what I'm told.

Now, I go to this garage every year. But one year they're busy, or I decide to shop around.

I come across a new garage. Similar deal but the reception seems to be more customer focused, there's a lot of information for the customer on what's what, how stuff works, how they fix things, which products they use and why, etc.

Plus, the wall behind reception is clear glass through which I can see my car being worked on. I can see the technicians protecting the sides of the car with padded blankets, doing their work with care, using brand name oils and filters, going what seems to be that extra mile.

It's an extra mile the last place would likely have claimed they do if I'd asked, the difference is I couldn't see it.

Furthermore, in the new place, if I have questions, I can talk to the technician doing the work.

The car is made ready, and I get my bill. It says the same sort of thing on my bill as the other garage. And I didn't see them do anything that the first garage didn't *claim* to do either.

The only real difference that I can *see* is that the bill is 10% higher.

Which garage am I going to go to next time around?

100% the new more expensive one.

The reason is simple: I can *see* they care about me, about the thing I care about, the thing I entrusted them with.

I have more confidence that the work is being done and being done well. Paying 10% less isn't a saving if I have 50% less confidence in the work being done or being done well.

10% more to feel like that I'm getting far superior service, service I am 100% confident in, that what matters to me is in good hands. It's a bargain. *I feel good about it.*

About a year and a half ago my employer received a tender request from a major strategic customer. They wanted to see what we as a company could deliver as opposed to our clients.

The questions were all functional. There was nothing about security, that would all be handled later by the "security people" with their checklists. No one really cared about that stuff.

The functionality we were being asked about involved this company, a global enterprise with a market cap of about one hundred billion dollars, sharing some significant intellectual property with whoever was going to win the tender.

No one at the customer interested in the functionality we were offering seemed to have considered the possible risks to their business of sharing that information. The same with the people managing the tender process.

In our reply deck, the security team added four slides which showed our assessment of the customer risk, why we took their security seriously, how the structure of our security team addressed those concerns, and the security stack we'd implemented to deliver.

They didn't ask, but we answered anyway.

I believe doing so makes a customer aware of the risk they are taking and creates an interest in that area. That means they'll now start considering that risk as part of the selection process, and sure enough, they'll start asking competitors, who didn't answer anything about security because it wasn't asked, exactly what they do.

Likely, the best those competitors can then do is show an ISO certificate or similar. They could probably not answer specific questions with the level of detail we had provided up front in a time frame or with a level of consistency and detail that instilled any confidence.

Our level of concern about our customers didn't just make us look good, it raised questions which made our competitors look *bad*. And we'd shaped the psyche by showing them how their data was really important, doubling the psychological positive effect of our security, and doubling the negative impact of what now appeared to be a lack of concern [about something we'd highlighted was so important] from our competitors.

It also shows a level of insight into the finer intangibles that many people, including our customers, didn't think of. That positioned us as *leaders*. Not just in security, but in our whole space, because we considered the minutia of things (like security) that others hadn't.

We also showed a level of care in doing something (security) that people traditionally don't even look at.

This leaves the assumption that our functional (customer-visible) work must be just as good or even better.

Guess what? We were smaller, less established, but we got the business.

Brand Value

Brand value is something that's hard to define. It's a term that often gets thrown around without a clear benefit, but it's something that can straddle many advantages.

The more you can do in terms of security, especially when it's in a relatable way, the more you can play on customer loyalty, whether that be B2B or B2C.

Most B2B business will be backed by some due diligence (though usually poor in my experience) but a very strong security brand can make you top of mind for certain business customers regardless.

When it comes to B2C, brand perception is everything and can heavily influence decision-making.

The example of the tender situation and the garage analogy in the previous chapter are just two ways the security function can amplify brand value.

At the company in the tender situation, we had a Security Commercial Officer who, among his many duties, promoted marketing content around what we did for security and how it related to our customers. I'm not sure what the price of gold is right now, but he was worth his weight in it.

A strong security message around your brand isn't just a competitive advantage that it would be a shame to waste, but it's one that's amplified with every news story about a breach, and one that can be re-leveraged by Marketing each time there is a story in the news.

It also helps strengthen security culture within your organisation.

The more external security messaging you have and the more your customers come to you because of your security message, the more your internal staff understands that security is about a lot more than internal IT.

It's something customers come to you for, which makes it something everyone needs to support. It also means it's top of mind more often, and raises a powerful realisation within our biggest internal sceptics: if our customers think this stuff is important enough to come to us over, shouldn't we recognise its importance too?

The key is to make it relevant and have benefit to whichever party you are targeting.

Making It Relevant

"The key is to make it relevant and have benefit to whichever party you are targeting."

I want to elaborate on the last sentence of the last chapter. This will be a very short chapter, but I felt it deserved its own chapter regardless.

A big part of selling security internally, by which I mean arguing the case for it (hopefully in a way that benefits the business), is to *sell* it.

Selling is something I've only really discovered over the last few years of my career.

I've argued plenty, starting with weak arguments where it was mostly just me thinking it was important, to some fairly good business cases with financials that made sense.

But arguing isn't selling.

Selling is something different altogether. And selling requires different messages to different people.

Your Legal department needs a different argument than your Marketing department, your Sales Department, your IT, your Engineering department, Finance, and so forth.

And you also sell to *people*. Not necessarily the merits of the case.

Your proposals should absolutely be logical and have merit, of course. But understand the fact that those points may not be what *sells* said proposal.

Understanding and catering to the personal goals and preferences of the people you are targeting will have a huge impact on the effectiveness of your pitch.

The people involved have personalities, interests, preferences, values, drivers.

To achieve what *we* want, we must understand what *they* want.

Quality Business Benefits

In closing out this section of the book about quality, I want to briefly touch on something one more time as several examples have been given already.

We've seen how treating security vulnerabilities as quality defects helps us reduce how many we have over time, and hence lowering the odds of us being breached over time.

We can do this through well-established quality management principles used in other industries.

But we also know that while most security issues are quality defects, not all quality defects are security issues.

And, by addressing quality as the root cause of these security issues, we often end up benefitting other areas.

Improved structuring of tools and accounts can result in license savings and productivity gains.

Visibility to application usage can also lead to license savings.

Visibility to assets can improve the effectiveness and coverage of a wide range of IT services and find yet more savings.

Improving architectural and development standards can lead to more efficient systems, better stability, greater scalability, more agility, and significantly reduced compute costs.

Addressing cultural, organisational, and other issues ultimately behind security challenges can raise employee satisfaction and productivity by reducing friction and frustration.

All these things either have direct measurable impacts on the bottom line or are well known by management teams to drive improvements.

And that means more benefit for the business, and more traction for us.

Part Five – Executive Context

While many security practitioners aspire to be a CISO, I believe few appreciate what it means to be a true C-level, and therefore how to deal with other C-levels.

I see more and more efforts to remediate these shortcomings with an increasing number of courses and voices advocating for better communication, business focus, leadership skills, and so on. And while still tiny, this is a positive trend.

One thing I rarely see discussed though is the executive mindset. As such I wanted to write something about how, based on my experience anyway, I feel executives see us, what they care about, how we see them, and what ultimately motivates many of them.

I suspect these next few chapters may be uncomfortable but necessary for some practitioners, but also eye-opening for those who rarely think about the cold hard realities of business.

Executive Perception

I mentioned earlier that, while at a roundtable full of executives a few years ago, the most common answer given as to why they funded their security functions was "To make them go away."

I can't think of anything more alarming, or a bigger indicator of how disconnected most security functions are from the very businesses they are supposed to protect. Which means they can't.

The fact is that some security organisations are not being funded because they are effective, make sense, or have solid arguments and strategies to help the business be secure.

They are funded instead because of a lot of loud messaging that executives often do not understand but feel pressured by, and because the security functions are so awkward or confusing to deal with that management simply prefer *not* dealing with them. And that can mean just giving them money to make them go away, or not engaging with (or funding) them at all.

And I'm willing to bet that when I just said "messaging that executives often do not understand", the majority of security practitioners immediately thought that was executives' fault for "not understanding cyber".

Consider instead the fact that myopically overcomplicating something beyond the point of comprehension, especially with an approach that, at a macro level at least, goes against common sense, *does not make us special.*

To the contrary, it makes our competence, certainly to a senior executive, questionable. As a result, they are sceptical, and for good reason.

I assure you, I've been there, I've foolishly thought the same way, had that security rockstar syndrome, and I now firmly believe we have it backwards. It's often us "security people" that don't have a clue here.

Firstly, we're generally not great at communicating or influencing and that's going to hurt any way you slice it.

Secondly, as shown by the trends, our current [so-called] "risk-based" approach is mostly intangible, without accountability, and arguably ineffective overall due to the many factors already mentioned.

We then ask for more resource to do more of the same when just about every market trend indicates things are getting worse despite increased spending.

We can rarely present it in a way that makes sense to the stakeholders. To outsiders, this looks bad. And quite frankly it should look bad to us as practitioners too. Sometimes I feel we're too busy giving each other "cyber awards" to notice.

I'll go as far as argue that some security functions cause more "damage" (in terms of cost) to the organisations they're supposedly protecting than whatever they claim to be protecting them against. In as much as they've even managed to reduce the impacts of those things anyway.

I've seen organisations where I'm confident they'd have better overall security postures if they got rid of their security functions altogether and instead just had accountability about the quality of the IT department's outputs.

The only question is whether this is a small minority of security departments, or a worrying majority. My impression, based on my personal experience with the structure of security functions I've seen, is that it's significant. As is the waste.

Now, I know that in security-land, the likely response to that is "But you're forgetting that we stop the breaches!"

A few things here.

We don't really know if we stop the breaches as it's rather hard to measure anything that didn't happen without a comparison point. In fact, many organisations not spending anything on "security" don't suffer breaches and vice versa. So this is mostly ideological.

Remember the gun control argument? A lot of the people arguing that their brand of security prevented breaches would laugh people out of the room for suggesting more guns deterred crime. Yet here, when it benefits them, they're happy to make essentially the same argument.

However, just like with that gun control argument, we can look at the macro trends, and they're not good.

Things in security are getting worse, not better, the more we push the very agenda we say will make it better. And they're consuming an unsustainably increasing percentage of business's resources.

Even if we argue that we are reducing breaches thanks to all this spend, we cannot realistically claim that it's cost effective (every year has more spend and more breaches, remember?), or that it's the most effective way of going about it. Maximising that effectiveness is our financial responsibility to the business.

Communication plays a huge role here too. I've recently had someone comment that only regulatory pressure with massive fines would motivate executives to take security seriously. Which to me just shows how spectacularly bad we are at justifying and/or communicating the supposed cost of poor security to the business.

We admit that the risk of fines is considered, virtually all other risks presented to the business by other departments are considered, why do we think "our" risks aren't? Clearly the business is able to understand risks, so why do we need regulations to present a quantifiable risk in our stead? Are our risks even real? Does what we are offering make sense, financially or otherwise? If it was as dangerous to the business as we claim, wouldn't the business act?

On that note, I've also seen more than my share of *overstated* security risks. By which I mean the financial values given to the risk by security teams who often have little understanding of the business process that would be affected.

Indeed, when those risks come through, most businesses tend to suffer significantly lower losses than those estimated by the security teams, and most of the time they tend to be barely noticeable on the next quarterly report.

It's not just that the numbers are sometimes inflated to increase the perceived importance of the security function (and therefore of funding it), or the fact that many of the estimates are made without fully understanding the business process and revenue dynamics. It's also the failure to consider the resilience and ingenuity of the people involved in whatever business process was affected. I'll repeat it again: we may think we're "special" in security, but we are not.

The reality is that the people in roles more closely connected to the business's operations are likely better positioned than us when it comes to helping it overcome undesirable events.

Furthermore, it's my personal experience from coming in after breaches is that the risks raised by security are rarely the ones that fundamentally caused the incident.

All this to say that none of these things make us look good to senior management. But I suspect that in many cases things would be even worse if there was more transparency.

Getting that transparency is what I do when I help cyber insurers out of paying claims.

Presenting the resulting findings of obvious security negligence to the victim organisations. The resulting silence and disbelief from their management teams (some of which had invested heavily in "security") can be deeply awkward.

Even more uncomfortable is when these findings are shared with the security teams themselves. The sad part is that a lot of them, due to a myopic focus and lack of understanding of the big picture, genuinely thought they were doing a good job.

I know these comments aren't going to win me any popularity contests, but we are here to do a job and we need to get real about it.

I'm personally tired of hearing complaints about people not understanding how tough cybersecurity is, how misunderstood we are, how we should be paid more, and so forth when so many security functions out there are delivering poor results, can't quantify their value, and would shirk at the requirement to do so.

Don't get me wrong. There are some genuinely gruelling roles out there where people are trying to hold things together. But they are usually a result of poor leadership in place, and that includes the leadership of many CISOs.

We need to shake this sense of "specialness" in security and start driving real accountability for ourselves.

That lack of accountability not only keeps us from being self-aware enough to drive the right solutions, but it can make it hard for the business to understand us, what we do, and to trust us.

I mentioned earlier how the hardest part of my job is getting the right people, often an executive, to listen to me.

This is due to all the reasons mentioned in this chapter. The perception we've created makes them simply not want to talk to me because I'm "security".

There is distrust and even disdain of "security people" at a level I don't think most people even realise. And it's there for good reason whether practitioners realise it or not.

Conversely, the *easiest* part of my job talking to those same people once they realise that I'm not the "security person" they were expecting.

It's amazing the amount of traction I get just calling out the status quo – how much executives are willing to talk about, and interested by, security the moment you stop talking about it like a "security person".

And that should be a damning wake up call to us all.

The Business' Concern

In the previous chapter I mentioned the security argument of "But we stop the breaches!"

I believe there is one more important point on why this argument may not be beneficial to us in terms of executive engagement and communication:

The business may not, ultimately, *care* about breaches.

And if you, as a senior C-level security leader think that's a problem, then you may find you have missed the point entirely, in the hard, bottom-line, Wallstreet sort of way, about why you are doing security for your business.

In many ways, breaches don't actually matter. What matters is money. That's just business.

It's noteworthy that many businesses started caring significantly more about breaches after regulations came in where they could be heavily fined if they didn't. That just goes to show that, when it was left purely down to the economics of breaches, having a breach wasn't considered that big of a deal.

(In many cases it still isn't, despite the increasing cost of ransomware attacks. About which, incidentally, I haven't seen any conclusive data that shows security spending is reducing...)

I still see statistics from security vendors saying anywhere between 35% and 85% of businesses were hit with a security breach last year. However, the percentage of those businesses that failed or were grievously impacted financially as a result is *tiny*.

And this is, partly, why operational activities, projects, initiatives, and in fact almost *anything* that drives the bottom line will always take priority over today's mainstream security practices.

To me that's yet another reason why security should be practiced as a quality function which creates savings and efficiencies by improving the outputs of all business functions, rather than a separate cost-centre always trying to mitigate defects, and often slowing things down.

In short, sure, security is important. But not at the expense of the bottom line.

And yes, granted, the cost of breaches is going up. Partly due to regulation and fines, and partly due to the current direction of layering on security technologies while allowing organisations to become more vulnerable over time underneath due to neglecting root causes and scaling up problems.

But if we cannot justify, measurably, that we are improving the bottom line (without deluding ourselves), why are we here? Let me rephrase that, why would *the business* want us here?

To me, it's one more reason why it's so critical to not "do security", but to strategically move the organisation's way of working to such a state where it needs as little of today's operational "security" work [and its associated costs] as possible.

To where there is a clear and obvious net financial benefit from our efforts, and ideally while achieving other contributions to the bottom line.

That, I feel, is what the business cares about.

Our Perception of the Executive

What about our side's perception of business executives?

I've seen many security practitioners (and LinkedIn memes) lament how the CISO is a C-level position and should therefore report to the Board, be granted significant budget and authority, and so forth. They often paint executives that don't give the security department whatever it wants in a negative light, even ridiculing them.

I think these people miss the point entirely. In fact, I feel that this mindset can make these security practitioners detrimental to the organisation (and its bottom line).

Denigrating senior management is simply not what we should be doing. Not only are most executives there for a reason, but this sort of sentiment is counterproductive to achieving the traction we need to succeed.

That toxic attitude I see demonstrated in many practitioners, especially those that fancy themselves as "security leaders", towards senior leadership is also a sign of very poor leadership competency in of itself. These people are expecting the privilege without any of the work or obligation.

(While I may be slating "security leaders" a bit here, I'm willing to bet the good ones are nodding in agreement!)

So, let's talk about that senior management.

Let's start with the common expectation that they must understand cyber security and all the technology and concepts we've created in our current approach, which seems particularly absurd considering the abysmal performance of that very approach. It's debatable whether we ourselves even understand what works best.

I'm also bolstered in this view by the sheer number of CISOs I've come across who push back against visibility and accountability. Those who demand much but are willing to account for little.

We have lots of little approaches and technologies for tackling individual symptoms of poor security in our IT and business processes, but we're historically not great at structuring a holistic approach that solves the underlying problem.

More pertinent perhaps is that all other departments (many of whom have concepts as alien to us as security is to them) manage to make themselves understood just fine. And I see a lot of people thinking it's because we're somehow special. Are we? Or are we just bad at communicating?

Now is a good time to mention something which I believe is a key definition, for me anyway, of a C-level role.

A C-level does not just direct the department(s) they own. They have the whole business at heart and work to influence it in its *entirety* to ensure maximum synergy across *all* departments.

They do this for the benefit of the entire business. Not their individual department. The wider business comes first.

How they help the organisation realise value by optimising how *all* parts of the business work together in collaboration with other executives and leaders, is the true measure of a great C-level in my book.

How they run their own department(s) is important, but secondary. The ability to work together with others is a bigger factor to the overall success of the business than excellence within any specific silo.

Doing this means they can shape the business so that their function can work [cost] effectively, as opposed to chasing huge amounts of resource to mop up, mitigate, and firefight incompatible output from other departments.

As you can imagine, this need to shape the entire organisation at a senior level puts communication, altruism, and the ability to influence high up on the list of essential skills and attributes for such a person.

Those mocking executives for "not getting" cyber are unlikely to have these skills, or even a basic understanding of what drives business success.

I believe that when some "security people" complain that the CEO or Board "doesn't get it" it is far more likely that it is them who don't get it.

They don't understand the business priorities, haven't taken the time to learn how departments operate, what they need, what matters to them, and how to communicate it all in a way that not only makes sense to the business, but also *appeals* to it.

I.e.: Not "We need to buy [more] CyberBlinkyBox 9000 devices... Because baddies!!" because that means nothing to the business. And yet you'd be amazed at how many "security strategy" documents I get that amount to little more than this.

I feel there is still a significant lack of thinking about what's important for the business to succeed from the part of security practitioners, and more importantly, "security leaders".

I'm still seeing what could be considered infantile discussions about whether a CISO "should be technical."

We should be so far past that by now.

If a CISO is to be a true C-level role, then the CISO needs to have high level understandings of Finance, Legal, HR, Marketing, Product Design, Sales, Strategy, IT, and just about everything else covered in an MBA course to understand and communicate with their C-level peers.

A good technical understanding is of course useful in helping to understand technological issues, but at C-level you're realistically far too busy with formulating strategy and staying on top of and influencing the business for the technical knowhow to get much use.

In my case that technical knowledge serves mostly to help me identify competent technical leaders I can delegate to.

But regardless of how you feel about it, the fact that we spend orders of magnitude more time in security circles arguing about the needed level of "techie-ness" than we do discussing business understanding and senior management traits is telling.

I think a basic level of business immersion and education would do us security practitioners a lot of good not only in terms of personal development but also in being able to understand, engage, and communicate so that we may drive better results.

Executive Motivation

Now, with that out of the way, let's talk about executive *motivation.*

If we are to communicate and work effectively with people at the senior-most levels of business, we need to understand what motivates them.

We need to realise what they're in it for.

In most cases, it's *money.*

A significant number of founders and an even higher percentage of the executives they hire aren't that fussed with what the company does. They care that it runs well and makes money.

Moreso, they're probably looking to sell the business or their stake in it. I.e.: They think about their personal exit strategy before they even start or join the business.

Which, incidentally, means they may not care at all about a risk that is five years away, because it may not even be their risk if they plan to exit three years from now.

Their ultimate responsibility is to themselves and (hopefully) to their stakeholders/shareholders.

They want to grow valuations, pipelines, and EBITDAs, anything that will amplify the value of their and their shareholders' stake(s) in the company.

So, while they may collect a salary, the bulk of their compensation will be in *equity*.

And you don't grow the value of your equity by building big teams and spending loads of money on fancy toys. That is how you *lower* EBITDA numbers, which is *bad* for valuations.

Now imagine a CISO wants to do just that (build big teams and buy a lot of tools) but doesn't seem to really know a whole lot about the organisation's value proposition, exit timeline, and isn't able to articulate *why* this money should be spent in terms of hard financial return.

Consider what we've said previously about breaches rarely being *that* damaging to the balance sheet and realise how that requested "security" might irk the leadership (and shareholders) who are building the value of their equity, while the CISO's running costs that will lower it.

It's like having a friend that keeps doing things that end up costing *you* money without them realising it; that sense of increasing frustration you have with them.

Consider value multipliers in valuations and 2-10% equity positions for some execs... A seven-figure annual security budget could *personally* cost each executive you're trying to convince that much money at exit time due to its impact on EBITDA and valuation, let alone actual cost.

Could you, as a security practitioner honestly say that you will generate more than 100% ROI for the business out of what you're asking?

If it came down to it, would you be willing to fund it *out of your own personal pocket* trusting you'll get your money back and more?

I hope that highlights some of the reason why they may be reluctant to fund something they do not understand and can't be measured, especially when more effective, relatable, and easily communicable methodologies such as those we've been discussing are available.

Friction is only natural when security has some big asks, costing stakeholders a lot of money, without a clear financial upside.

That is why a commercial mindset, being altruistic to be business rather than to the security status/clique, and the ability to at least relate to an executive mindset are so important in my opinion.

It's one more way in which the quality-focused approach (with its many cost benefits) and the thoughts on commercialising security shared previously can help us.

They are not just more relatable and appreciable to an executive audience but can also *excite* them due to the prospect of increasing the business' bottom line for its stakeholders and themselves.

And that, in my mind, is our best way of getting a seat at the table and the traction to deliver our security programmes.

And maybe a nice chunk of equity as well.

On From Here...

There is, of course, much more to be said. And probably a lot more for me to learn and hopefully share back to the community in the future.

There will never be a comprehensive guide to security, it permeates everything, and as such the possibilities go on forever.

But we have to draw a line somewhere I've ostensibly reached the end of what I wanted to share, for now.

For the most part I hope the observations, concepts, and points of view I've shared help you achieve your goals and, more importantly, inspire new ideas in you that can move all of us forward.

But before saying goodbye, I want to share a few more things with you.

For starters, I received a lot of queries after writing *Rethinking InfoSec* on how I personally structured security programmes. I've since refined how I do this quite a bit and in Appendix A you'll find a 50-page write-up explaining the structure of the last programme I built. This is for you to use as a guidance or inspiration to do your own thing should you wish to do so.

Another thing I want to leave you with, in Appendix B, is of course the Hitachi Vantara blog series I mentioned at the start of this book (and to which this first edition of What We Call Security owes its existence).

While the blog's goal was to show just how storage and recovery (and associated capabilities) are relevant to security in ways most have not considered, it also features some great examples of how different thinking can breed entirely new concepts and approaches.

Finally, in this book we've touched on culture, marketing, finance, leadership, strategy, operations, product engineering, quality, critical thinking, even character.

You may have noticed that I mostly pointed out and complained about the problems we have around these things. While I hope the correct behaviours we should be adopting instead are obvious, I did not actually explore them much. I've also not gone into much depth on most of the aforementioned areas and disciplines either.

There's a couple of reasons for that. For one, it's not the goal of this book, but more importantly I'm also by no measure the best person to speak about them.

Instead, I am going to leave you with a reading list of books on these topics, written by people far more qualified than myself.

These are the books I've had on the top shelf of my bookshelf for the last year or two. They've helped me dramatically progress my thinking and my career, and I strongly recommend you read them after this book in the hope that they do the same for you.

The Five Dysfunctions of a Team – Patrick Lencioni

The Advantage – Patrick Lencioni

This Is Marketing – Seth Godin

The Personal MBA – Josh Kaufman

How to Win Friends and Influence People – Dale Carnegie

Good Strategy Bad Strategy – Richard Rumelt

The Goal – Eliyahu Goldratt & Jeff Cox

The Challenger Sale – Matthew Dixon & Brent Adamson

The Subtle Art of Not Giving a F*ck – Mark Manson

The last one may come as a surprise to some.

For those unfamiliar with it, I believe the title to be somewhat misleading. I consider it to be primarily about self-awareness and self-accountability.

These are essential for us doing the right thing and becoming good leaders (and good people), not to mention being able to endure. It is arguably the most important book on the list.

I personally found it eye-opening and think it should be part of every school curriculum. It's even helped me sleep better.

Read it first.

And on that note, it's time for me to say goodbye and leave you to the appendices.

I hope you've found this book helpful.

Even if you disagreed with it or parts of it, I hope it's helped you consider different perspectives or sparked new ideas.

The important thing is for us to move forward, and to realise that we can't do that until we've found the right direction. We must admit when we're lost and take the time to work out what our true destination is and how to reach it.

Thank you for reading, and good luck.

Appendix A – Building Security Programmes

As mentioned, a lot of people have asked me how I build frameworks and programmes over the last few years. I'm therefore happy to finally put something a little more detailed on how I do that.

One thing you'll notice about this framework is that, beyond ensuring we have a defined strategy, securing management support, and the ensuring the needed connection points within the organisation are defined, a lot of it is based on systematically going through applications, systems, IT and business processes, and so forth. "Doing security", as in operational security work and "cyber" technologies play only a very small role.

It's easy to get tightly focused on each individual area as we work through things, but please remember that we should always have the business and the quality of its [business and IT] outputs in the back of our mind.

That, more than anything, should define what is needed in our programme and with what granularity.

Programmes vs Frameworks

I often use the terms Programme and Framework interchangeably, but I would roughly define them as follows:

A security programme is the body of work delivering everything we do in our service to the organisation.

The security framework is the structure needed to document, define, and organise that body of work.

The "document" and "define" parts are particularly important and often overlooked. They serve not just in defining security operations (where many security functions stop) but also provide written guidelines and agreements for our interactions with *other* parts of the business, including activities *they* must do.

Now I want to immediately clear up that my concept of a security framework is *not* implementing ISO 27001, NIST, or anything similar for the reasons highlighted previously in this book.

For me a framework is a structured container containing all the elements of a programme designed to meet the specific security needs of *our* organisation and its specific business processes.

Note that I didn't say IT or infrastructure. Those are merely elements that support our organisation's business processes. We must focus on business process first. This will naturally lead us to the supporting elements which include technology ones.

I first started building frameworks like this about ten years ago with the goal of overcoming a number of problems I saw in the delivery of work by security teams.

Lots of policies, processes, jobs, tasks, functions, tools, but their application and execution always seemed to be, if I'm being kind, "a bit messy". And messy leads to gaps that let bad things happen.

Accepting this is a bit like putting your precious tropical fish in an aquarium that only has a few small cracks and holes. You may as well just dump them on the floor because the end result will be the same.

More worrying was the fact that a lot of the work I was seeing was piecemeal not just in systems and processes, but even with entire departments. And there seemed to be little effort invested in making sure there was visibility and awareness across the business.

Security programmes should be delivering a foundation of integrity onto which we can build, but they rarely if ever do. Instead of a foundation, many try to "layer on" security too late in the game and I feel it is the reason behind so many of the failures I've seen.

I had made a list of some of the key issues I saw at the time around why I felt most programmes failed to deliver:

- A lack of general organisation.
- Tick-box implementations of individual technologies without further consideration.
- No clear definition of activities.
- An impossibility to consistently enforce processes.
- A lack of detail in processes and policies.
- Loose and scattered pieces of documentation (Policies, processes, standards, etc.) with no inventory.
- No systematic and holistic approach in documenting operations.
- Leaving many IT processes with heavy security impacts up to IT with no review of their efficacy.
- A tendency for processes not being well aligned to each other.
- Process/work duplication due to a lack of integration.
- Process outputs not feeding into other processes and processes and registries consequently going out of sync.
- References to documents and policies no one can locate because they weren't considered and updated in conjunction with the documents referencing them.
- Documents often out of date.
- Documents in conflict with each other (even if in small ways) because they come from different sources or were written under different contexts without considering the big picture.
- The list goes on...

As mentioned, the list above was from about ten years ago. While I think it still highlights many valid points, it also highlights my own lack of thought maturity at the time.

You may have noticed the strong IT focus. For example, If I were to do it over again today, I would change "Leaving many IT processes with heavy security impacts up to IT with no review of their efficacy."

With/to

"Leaving many *business* processes with heavy security impacts up to *other departments* with no review of their efficacy."

Basically, I'd rescope all of these to focus on the business process(es) and not just IT as I did back then.

It's also worth noting the implementation of the first framework I built was an abysmal failure.

The reason being that on my list of key issues I missed a massive one: The support of senior management. Getting that support would require defining it, creating a mandate to justify it, and laying out a strategy to deliver it. And then learning to communicate and sell it.

And that was when all I wanted to do was affect change in how IT operated, let alone the whole business like I do today!

Building a Framework

On to how I like to build such a thing...

Firstly, I want to touch on the fact that there are many frameworks used by information security teams/departments out there. We named ISO 27001 and NIST in the previous chapter, for example.

While many of the concepts within those frameworks are useful it's important to realise that they are neither strategies nor programmes. Why? Because they are simply not about *our* business, not beyond its most generic IT parts anyway.

The other problem I have with them is how they are implemented. If one requires something like authentication, for example, then I often see people implement *some* authentication... *somewhere*. It's often not done in a way that's measured to the business process it's authenticating, and often not holistically. We miss places, systems, and processes, but then tick the box because we have *some* authentication, again, *somewhere*.

Our security programme should reflect our business, it should implement our strategy which is, again, all about our business.

Doing it this way not only makes it a lot more effective from a risk perspective, but it also provides significant additional business benefits as discussed earlier this book. These benefits are completely missing from third-party compliance standards.

Worse still I see lot of resource taken away from helping the business actually be more secure for the sake of servicing compliance in ways that have questionable benefit.

I dare anyone that's participated in audit preparations where risk ratings in spreadsheets are being tweaked to show progress and evidence to the auditor is selectively collected in order to pass to tell me they feel their organisation is more secure than if they'd actually put that effort towards securing things.

And if you're reading this without having any first-hand experience of this, I can anecdotally tell you this is how it works most of the time. Sometimes security teams are pressured into being complicit, but they are also at times very much responsible, embracing this as standard practice.

It's a good example of so many things wrong with how security is done today and how we are failing the trust of our organisations, our partners, and our customers.

It's why I wanted to do things differently, hence taking a different approach on building programmes and frameworks that work for the business, not the status quo.

So, without further ado, let's look at what such a framework looks like.

The first thing I do is draw a box. Think of it as a container in which we put the elements needed to establish and run a successful programme.

The purpose of this is simple: to put everything in one place. *Everything* lives within this first "outer" box in one way or another.

Note that this will include any relevant components belonging *other* departments too. We will define those together with the relevant teams as to shape them to be secure, then keep them (or a link to them) in the box.

These components are procedures, standards, policies, processes, etc. We relate to them as documents. We have to be very careful to not think that they are just documents though. They are not. They are actions, operations, and rules. But they do have to be documented, and that means documents.

So, our framework is a collection of documents. Making sure those documents get actioned and actioned properly is a big part of the framework's purpose.

I have yet to see a single Information Security organisation effectively manage process documents. In 20 years of doing this, not one I've taken over or faced off with could provide an exhaustive listing of all InfoSec operational and process documents when asked, or maintain them up to date, or approved. Document management system or not.

Within that outer box I then create a number of other essentially horizontal boxes which I place one below the other like a stack so that my outer box ends up becoming a bit of a tall rectangle over time.

These boxes are the "domains" that make up the different areas of consideration I've found to be necessary to have a successful security programme.

What these boxes represent and what they contain has evolved over time and will continue to do so. They can also vary by business type.

I used to call them layers because of how they presented on paper in the diagrams of the framework, but this is a bit of a misnomer as there's no up or down dependency or interaction in the "stack" they form. They're effectively groupings, sometimes in concept, sometimes just for ease of management.

Anyway, albeit also imperfect, let's stick with the term "domains" for these.

As a working example, here's how I'd now structure the domains in a framework for a SaaS B2B services company like the one I worked for in my last CISO role.

After a lot of thought, I might eventually settle on these 11 domains (boxes) within my big box, to group the entirety of my programme:

1. Executive
2. Programme Definition
3. Interdepartmental Integration
4. IT Operations
5. SaaS & Business Applications
6. Product and Engineering
7. Human Factors
8. SecOps
9. Compliance
10. Commercial
11. Business Stubs

I want to repeat that this structure is entirely arbitrary and that you should feel very free to deviate.

In fact, I strongly recommend you do. The example here includes consideration for the specific sector, culture, maturity, and other factors of the organisation. The approach for a different organisation (like yours) should absolutely look at least a little different.

Now let's look at what these domains mean.

1. Executive: This always includes an Executive Charter that defines hard rules for the scope, responsibility, and authority of the security function, to be signed by the senior management team (the perfect place to pitch the security as quality concept and its many business advantages).

The other key document is a Security Strategy (business-centric, so well beyond IT) that explains and justifies the approach (including the framework), team structure, timelines, etc. involved in delivering it.

This is critical. You need a business-aligned security strategy, and you need real executive support. Many organisations have neither.

2. **Programme Management**: An overview of the whole programme, inventory of its components, continuous improvement process, how the activities will be scheduled and tracked.

3. **Interdepartmental Integration**: Define how we work together with various relevant but non-technical departments such as HR, Legal, Sales, and more to support our security strategy.

4. **IT Operations**: Define how we do everything IT related, from provisioning users, asset management, patching, architecture, backups, recovery, logging, email, networking, endpoint hardening, database configuration, media handling, cloud standards, change management, etc. This one tends to be quite large and could easily be broken into several sub-domains for ease of delegation or organisation. The important part is to define, in detail, with the relevant stakeholders, how each IT activity should be done with security in mind.

5. **SaaS & Business Applications**: Define the state in which every internally hosted or SaaS business application should be in to ensure security, one at a time, working with the stakeholders to understand the business processes, data, and potential impacts.

6. **Product and Engineering**: If applicable, define all the practices that should go into your product development, product security features, hosting/engineering environment, internal and external-facing product security documentation, etc.

7. **Human Factors**: This is where we drive cultural change (which is *not* the same as user awareness) in conjunction with HR, connect with stakeholders and the general workforce, and well work on process engineering to reduce elements of human error in business and IT processes.

8. **SecOps**: This is where the stuff most people associate is security goes. SOC operations, EDR, anti-phishing vulnerability management, incident notification/response, threat intelligence, forensics, etc.

9. **Compliance**: I do not build my security according to any third-party compliance standard. I feel doing so is not only backwards in some ways but also likely to result in missed areas and ill-fitting implementations. Instead, my compliance is based on the application of the framework. I can then

easily map my security processes and mechanisms to *any* compliance standard with minimum effort (a great business agility advantage when entering new verticals or markets). This is where those mappings happen.

10. **Commercial**: Here we define how we capture contract schedules that relate to security, any customer facing services like security-status portals, how we help Sales accelerate the RFI process (including any documentation to give customers), our involvement in any contractual negotiations with an impact on security, and any marketing and branding material around how our security gives us an edge. (If we think security is important, why wouldn't we have it be a brand value or selling point?)

11. **Business Stubs**: A place to store all other departments' relevant business processes (or links thereto), which should be taken into consideration when creating every component of the framework in all the domains listed above.

I'll try to explain a bit more about the thinking behind each of these domains over the next few chapters.

I hope it helps you create your own or come up something even better suited for your needs.

The Executive Domain

This part of the framework is in many ways the most straightforward to create, but potentially also the most important. And while it's the first thing you should do, it's also one that requires insight and experience.

It defines and obtains management support for our mandate, proposes the strategy and programme, and also defines our authority.

For me it usually contains two documents.

They work together and could be one document, but I usually separate them mostly for ease of presentation purposes.

The first is the Executive Charter. It states our mandate, captures the acceptance and support needed for our strategy and programme, and gets management sign-off for us to deliver it.

The second I call the Security Strategy Overview. It's an explanation of our strategy, the benefits, how it will be delivered (the programme), what resources we need, it defines and explains the team we will build to deliver it (as well as the need for others to work with us and vice versa), and a rough timeline on delivery (something like a three-year plan).

These documents are absolutely critical to get the support and capability you need to be successful.

Many CISOs talk about fighting for more budget.

If the goal is to build a fiefdom for yourself, great.

But if our goal is to altruistically help the organisation, financially, from risk, etc., then traction is a far more valuable commodity. Plus, traction will naturally bring with it the budget you need.

Remember me saying that I saw at an event where a group of executives said the number one reasons they funded their security functions was "To make them go away."?

These documents, destined for your ExCo and Board, contain the answers they *should* have given to that question.

Presenting them is also an opportunity to be seen and stand out. To demonstrate that you are business-minded, strategic, have a wealth of insights, know what you are doing, speak their language, and are focused on *the business'* goals.

If you do this properly, they will support you in supporting them.

It's critical you get right. I recommend first spending a few weeks to understand the business, understand the culture, speaking to the different people, hearing the complaints, getting a feel for different departments, and understanding the business's strategy and goals, as a whole and per department.

Then look at the current issues, their root causes, foresee what challenges could arise in tackling them, and how to best prevent and address them. Think beyond risk. And when you do think about risk, make sure it's real and relevant to the business.

Remember not to be myopic about technology or get sucked into fixing technical problems because they appeal to us when their resolution isn't, in terms of priorities at least, what's best for the business.

Now formulate a strategy and build a programme, for your business. I cannot tell you how to do this. You are the best placed person to understand what this should look like for your organisation, but you must be objective and take the time to understand your business.

What I can help you with is in creating an Executive Charter which references your security strategy and programme.

(The fact that the Executive Charter tends to remain largely the same between organisations while the Security Strategy can change dramatically is another reason why I've split them as two documents in the Executive Domain of my frameworks.)

The inspiration for an Executive Charter came to me studying for my PMP certification about 15 years ago.

One of PMI's principles is that every project should have a Project Charter that defines the authority, resource, scope, budget, and so forth for a given project as to prevent that project being deviated, encountering scope creep, being defunded, having timelines changed, etc.

I saw clear benefits in such a charter in terms of addressing a lot of the challenges I faced in delivering a holistic security function.

The contents of an Executive Charter are mostly statements or directives for which we need executive level agreement and backing.

I typically include the following ten:

1. **Overall Responsibility**: Here we state that senior management accepts overall responsibility for Information Security.

   We then add that it is ultimately the responsibility of each team and department to ensure the security of its outputs with the guidance of the security functions.

   This is likely to be where you first encounter some surprise that "security" won't be sorting everything by itself and your first opportunity to explain the concept and value proposition of "security through quality" (which I like to elaborate on in my Security Strategy document).

2. **Mandate**: We state that management delegates the above responsibility to the Information Security function, with a clear scope and appropriate responsibility. This is also a good place to dictate that the function will report to the ExCo and Board in order to ensure they have enough information to fulfil *their* obligations under the previous point.

3. **Define Security Strategy**: How will InfoSec deliver? This is where we state that we will create and deliver an Information Security framework that will develop, disseminate, and enforce a cohesive set of processes and procedures as well as implementing technological security elements as needed. Leave this at a high level and refer to the more tailored and detailed Security Strategy document we talked about earlier.

4. **Authority**: Here we state that management grants the CISO and security team the necessary authority to apply and enforce all elements of the framework. Some organisations may have competing authorities, this is a good place to define hierarchies and priorities.

5. **Resources & Support**: Here we clearly state that senior management shall provide all reasonably necessary resources for the implementation of the above framework. If you have any ideas on how you can get management to demonstrate their support (and everyone else's expected

support) to the organisation, this is a good place to put them.

6. **Project Involvement**: I like to mention this one specifically because it's important to drive it through: we must be involved at the initial stages of projects in order to ensure a solid security foundation. So, let's state that management will instruct all project leaders to involve security from initiation. And no, that's not limited to IT.

    To avoid any issues with non-compliance to this, I like to include that management give explicit authority for the security function to request details on any aspect of any project at any time. We need to stipulate that we shall also be involved in any executive roadmaps and be able to impose any security gates necessary on projects and have a say at go-live time to make sure any risks are dealt with or acknowledged. By the way, we can always grant individual teams the authority to proceed if we trust them to implement.

7. **Control Over Change**: Pretty much the same as above, but for any operational changes. We must be able to review and approve/deny changes.

8. **Security Exceptions**: Here we state that we can be overruled. Let's face it, some people will always try to go over our heads. Even the most security savvy businesses can have a valid need to override

security standards and processes now and again. We should also not have unlimited powers either!

It's important that we allow for this and make sure it's done through a formal process. This adds not just accountability, but also predictability to exceptions which allows us to make them less frequent. If we don't set a clear path for these exceptions, they end up all over the place, unmanageable, and often undocumented.

9. **Visibility**: Here we state that the security function can request information about existing or new infrastructure, projects, applications, etc. This is essential to the application of security and the proactive discovery of issues and relevant business processes. We can now proactively investigate anything we have a hunch about, not just the new stuff rolling in.

   I also like to present the concept of "Direct Visibility" here, meaning we must be able to *directly* see the systems in the environment, without being dependent on IT as there can be political, cultural, and other reasons for security not being presented a true picture when asked.

10. **Daily Operations (security-relevant)**: This is where we define who has responsibility for security-relevant daily operations. This could be patching, backups, or any other activity associated with security or providing a foundation for security.

It's important for responsible parties to be identified and given the necessary resources and authorities too. They should also be added as signatories to the charter.

Once again, do feel free to modify any of these. Split them, remove some, add more. Do whatever it takes to best cover the underlying challenges you anticipate in *your* particular organisation. This is why it's so important to take the time to first get to know the organisation as thoroughly as possible before creating your charter.

Many of these directives are in place to make our future framework/programme functions properly. Only once you have a good idea of what your strategy is and what organisational, technical, cultural, and political problems you will face will you be able to write the executive charter that will make success possible.

Now let's fly through the rest of our framework domains...

The Programme Management Domain

This domain is dedicated to the management of the programme.

I came up with it because I observed that a lot of the security programmes that I came across suffered from being scattered or lacking upkeep. Even in the best cases, the continued management of scope and relevance was lacking, which resulted in parts of the business not being effectively protected.

I typically include four components:

1. Programme Overview
2. Continuous Improvement
3. Management System
4. Operations Schedule

The Programme Overview component presents the entire structure and a full inventory of all components. The idea being to have a full representation of all the components of the framework that leaves nothing else out.

It lists all documents in the programmed, their purpose, their last update, an illustration of the framework, as well as a recap of the strategy and structure of the team and stakeholders charged with executing it.

This document is what I usually hand to auditors, along with the charter and strategy documents mentioned before, to explain what we are doing and why.

I used to worry that they'd find it unconventional, but I've never had an auditor not be impressed with the thoroughness of the approach. Some have even asked if they could copy the template.

A little side story: In one organisation where security was several levels removed from the ExCo and Board, half the cover page by a report from our external auditors was about the promise presented by the programme they'd seen from me.

At that point the ExCo and Board didn't even know I or the programme existed. In fact, the CIO was resisting on signing off on the programme and I felt somewhat boxed in. But I did seize the opportunity presented by the auditor.

It wasn't long before the Board enquired, the security programme received the needed support, and I was on a first name basis with the Chief Exec... who offered me a ride in their McLaren. Which was nice.

The second component, the Continuous Improvement piece, defines how components (usually documents) are added, updated, and removed from the framework, the associated processes, frequency, how versioning is to be tracked, and so forth.

Its purpose is essentially to ensure the framework remains up to date, relevant, and efficient.

The third component, the Management System, defines just that. How will we manage the programme's framework.

A decade ago, the framework would have been a collection of documents in a folder and subfolders. Versioning would be done with folder hierarchy and file naming conventions.

Nowadays its far easier to build out the programme in something like Atlassian, where we can store all the documents in Confluence, and schedules and workflows in Jira allowing direct contributions, easy sharing, and much more.

The final component, the Operations Schedule is used to schedule all the operational elements. How often do you run your backups, your recovery tests, your incident response tabletop exercises, your vulnerability scans, and so on and so forth. I used to have a huge spreadsheet to track all this but obviously nowadays any number of planning and workflow solutions are a lot more powerful and flexible.

The Interdepartmental Integration Domain

This domain started out as an HR Integration domain when I wanted to define things HR would need to be involved in such as an Acceptable Use Policy, the definition of job roles for automated access provisioning purposes, a disciplinary process, investigations into employees, pushing improvements to culture, security training, and so forth.

It then grew to include the Legal department due to some legal issues and concerns around the above. That relationship with Legal grew to include GDPR, compliance, contractual issues with purchases, incident disclosure, making sure we considered any [security] liabilities in customer contracts, and generally reviewing anything the business was undertaking from a security liability perspective.

More than just dealing with potential legal issues, having an open dialogue with Legal also made us aware of a lot of things going on in the business due to Legal often being involved in some capacity.

As a bonus, the General Counsel tends to have a seat at Board/ExCo level and get listened to. A good relationship with them and their team can be a huge help getting traction and support for your programme.

In my last organisation, with a strong B2B focus and enormous multi-national customers, we started working closely with Sales and Product teams too in order to make sure that our delivery matched our commitments and to help guide what we (our business, not our security team) could achieve in terms of commercial promises around anything relevant to security.

I've found that helping commercial teams answer technical concerns from customers, especially time-sensitive ones, to help win business can really help build support for the security teams from a commercial perspective.

It won't surprise you to find that being seen as a contributor to the top line is a lot better than a drain on the bottom one.

All this to say that the purpose of this domain is to define the interactions, relationships, roles, and responsibilities between non-technical departments in delivering on the security strategy.

(The technical parts/aspects of the business have their own domains in my framework for ease of management purposes due to there being more items at play.)

So far, for me, this domain has focused on HR, Legal, and Sales, but you may find benefit to including other areas. Or to give those other areas their own dedicated domains like the next few I'll cover in the following chapters.

The IT Operations Domain

And now we're finally getting into the technical meat and potatoes of our framework.

This domain is where I put all IT operations and related/supporting processes, standards, and guidelines relevant to or needed for ensuring security.

I'll list some of the components I'd put here, in no particular order, without going into detail as these will vary significantly.

- Risk Management
- Change Management
- SDLC Security
- Asset Management
- Procurement Standards
- Systems/Instances Provisioning
- Data Retention
- Systems & Cloud Architectural Standards
- JML Process
- Configuration Management & Enforcement
- Patch Management
- Event Logging
- Email & Phishing
- Endpoint Security
- Backup & Recovery
- Network Security
- Vulnerability Assessments
- Guidelines for Cloud Services

- Mobile Device Management
- Disaster Recovery/BCP
- Incident Response & Notification
- Authentication Standards
- Media Sanitation & Disposal
- Supply Chain Security Standards
- Reporting Guidelines
- User Provisioning
- Documentation Standards
- Etc.

Hopefully that gives a general impression. Essentially, it's to document any process, policy, standard around running IT Operations (or anything that has a bearing on IT Operations like architecture) that are relevant to information security.

It tends to be, by far, the largest part of the framework. That said most of the actions, once defined, should be the responsibility of IT Operations and Engineering departments.

The main point being that it's important for operations (how we build and run things) to be well defined to ensure both security and consistency (a key element of quality) and not allow the kind of entropy that leads to vulnerabilities, unknowns, and even runaway or shadow environments.

Despite the importance of this, such operations are often not documented, documented poorly, or with lacking detail and granularity. They also often don't include security considerations.

Populating this domain is a great familiarisation exercise to better understand all our IT processes, mature their documentation, and insert security considerations so that they produce more repeatable, consistent, and secure outputs.

It's also probably the part of the framework that will take the longest to build out. It has the most components, requires the most outside assistance (but can also be the most delegated) of all the framework's domains.

Prioritise wisely.

The SaaS & Business Applications Domain

With the advent of cloud, more and more business applications have become cloud-based and therefore hosted on their own infrastructure and developed with their own standards and approaches.

This has led to me creating this domain for my programmes to individually address these applications.

The components are therefore all the SaaS applications used in the business.

I normally create one document per application with each presenting the business rationale and purpose of the application, a risk assessment, what data is processed or stored, the business importance and criticality, who would be using the application (and for what, if there are different levels of access or functionality).

The rest of each document defines, in detail, how the application should be configured. That includes the structure, the configuration, the user roles, associated permissions, and so forth.

The goal being here to force thought into how each application is used, make sure it's used securely, and to have all security-relevant elements be documented and tracked.

Components of this domain could include:

- Google Workspace
- Confluence
- Jira
- Miro
- Salesforce
- Etc.

To use Salesforce as an example, we would define the workflow, how access controls work, what sales information or contracts each user should have access to, what level of access should be granted, as well as anything else that needs to happen within the application to meet our broader policies around things like data retention/deletion or backups, for example.

Business applications built and hosted on-premises tend to have gone through more scrutiny than cloud-based ones. As such they are more likely to benefit from centralised services around things like updates and backups, but this isn't a given and as such I would still recommend creating a document for each one in this part of the framework.

I'll end with the personal observation that business applications, especially SaaS ones, are one of the biggest elements of unaddressed technology risk in a lot of organisations.

The use of these applications tends to serve business-focused functions, often handling sensitive and critical data such as sales information, financials, contracts, customer submitted data, payroll, internal data on staff, business plans, intellectual property, and more.

Yet, they often receive little to no attention as they are not a part of the core IT function, as well as sometimes being used by departments without the IT and security functions even being aware.

I hope that highlights not just the importance on focusing on these [SaaS] applications, but also of being familiar with all departments' business processes to identify which of these applications may be in use, where, for what, and by who in your organisation.

The Product & Engineering Domain

Product organisations are peculiar beasts.

The amount of flexibility (and lack of accountability) that some Engineering departments are offered in the name of accelerating innovation can be an absolute nightmare for the CISO.

And it's often not limited to security problems either, although the business is often unaware of the broader issues generated.

It usually comes down to a lack of architecture and code quality in that many Engineering functions seem to only be expected to deliver requested functionality, and fast.

Hundreds of random system instances generated then left unused, inefficient compute functions that inflict enormous excess cloud costs, code full of potential [and sometimes obvious] security vulnerabilities (and other unknowns), platforms that can make even the most hardened DevOps and Site Reliability Engineers pull their hair out... These are just some of the things rarely noticed by the business but that can make any concerned CISO stew with frustration. It's no surprise I've heard Engineering departments referred to as the "Fountain of Risk".

In terms of security being a quality function and helping reduce tangible business costs (beyond just reducing risk), getting involved in Engineering and Product is also probably the biggest contribution we can do.

It's also likely to be the one the business pushes back the hardest on, so communication on the benefits here is important. It's often the department where all deliverables are seen, but all the external costs it inflicts are not. We must present a larger picture where those costs are visible.

It's not limited to what we mentioned before either, all those things lead to technical debt, the need for more computing (costs), less stable applications, slower applications, more effort to remediate, and every new change or feature will become just a little more difficult, time consuming, and expensive to implement.

I've seen first-hand how poor engineering practices not only resulted in huge numbers of vulnerabilities, but also seven figure amounts of excess compute usage, cause change requests that should have taken days take months due to excess complexity, burnout and turnover in support staff, affected the viability and/or saleability of a product, and even bleed out a company's capital reserves forcing painful restructuring and layoffs.

There is also the issue that many product development engineers and managers are oblivious to client companies' expectations when it comes to security in a B2B context.

Combating this is the rationale behind this part of the framework.

So, let's quickly cover what I include in it.

The first thing is about product features: What minimum security features should the product have? For example, you may set a policy that all your products should be able to integrate with a third-party identity provider, have end-to-end encryption, store credentials with certain encryption mechanisms, feature MFA, and so forth.

After that I define that want full security documentation of each application which explains what platform it runs on, what the authentication mechanisms are, how data is stored, what the data flows are, how each function works, and so forth.

I typically want a detailed version for internal use and one to present to clients from both a pre-sales and due-diligence standpoint.

Other components can vary but will focus on ensuring the quality and consistency of development processes.

This can include guidelines or policies on which languages to use, rules around libraries, best practices around the use of GitHub, the overall development process, code reviews, general application security, testing regimes, and so on.

I think "Product" and "Engineering" could be treated as separate domains with one focusing on the product itself (functional [security] features) and the other one the quality and consistency of development (along with the associated best practices), but I've found that combining both has worked well as they complement each other in the psyche of the teams involved.

Plus, by exposing both Product and Engineering teams (when they are separate teams) to the same part of the framework, it can have the positive effect of helping them better understand each other's roles and obligations when it comes to security.

The Human Factors Domain

This is likely to be an unusual one for a lot of people as the field of human factors isn't one that's yet widely applied or recognised in most security functions.

The field of human factors relates to human error and behaviours. It deals with everything from training, understanding human behaviours, improving adhesion to instructions/processes, cultural change, and more.

How critical a focus on human factors will be in our security program is highly dependent on our business, particularly the level of organisational health. What we need from this function will also vary wildly based on the people and cultural challenges in our particular organisation.

As a result, I can only give you an example from my personal experience to give you a feel of what can be achieved.

In my last role as a CISO I employed such a human factors expert on the team. The core driver for this was the number of cultural problems within the organisation. This manifested itself in a lack of structure and discipline, distrust of management, resistance to change, and an unwillingness to accept outside criticism.

Plus, there had never been a security function in the organisation before, let alone one that wanted the change the way everyone operated, so resistance was expected.

The initial response to our expert was the same as it was to the rest of us: polite acceptance to our face, with back-channel communications of "Why are these people here? We have better things to do. Get rid of them."

Which was in many ways a reflection of the general culture at the time and no number of reports or plans was going to change that.

Instead, we tasked our expert, who was also a student of Fair Culture (worth a search if you are unfamiliar) to start picking random people to talk to and ask them about their work... and to show an interest.

The first thing this gave us, was lots of insights into what teams did. The next thing it did was build relationships, and trust so that people would share things with us. This in turn yielded some significant finds about processes not documented anywhere, sensitive data being used in places and ways that no one knew about, some really dangerous practices, and some of our most significant risks that technical solutions would have been unlikely to detect.

People manipulating production data using system accounts, entire undocumented environments with no controls testing with live data, 30 people using the admin account of a departed employee, code being left on internet repositories, and much more.

Assessing what training we needed and getting people to take it up was another responsibility. As was building up a positive, proactive, and altruistic culture throughout the business to ensure people would care enough to help us achieve our security goals.

That leads me to our human factors expert working side by side with HR to educate people around Fair Culture and promote its adoption.

In many ways our expert acted as my right arm when it came to creating relationships as I got too busy. A personal and hands-on approach (with people, not tools) has always been something I strive for, but you quickly reach a point where it's no longer possible to have regular interaction with everyone or even every team.

Another critical aspect of human factors is human error and process engineering.

The first part aims to determine why people make mistakes and rectify the root causes. This can be a poor culture with a slapdash approach to things (or even contempt), poor training, unclear processes (due to badly formatted instructions, ineffective distribution, or even misunderstandings due to cultural differences), management pressures, personal difficulties, inadequate tools, confusing systems, and any number of other factors.

Process engineering involves making sure processes, whether they are instructions, mechanisms to distribute those instructions, prompts on a form, etc., are optimised in such a way (including psychologically) to minimise human errors, and maximise people's inclination to perform the task as intended rather than avoid or shortcut it.

Whether you need a human factors component as part of your security strategy, programme, and framework up to you, but I believe it can be of significant value.

I'll sum it up as follows:

Security, or quality, is about defining the desired state and maintaining that state. As I mentioned in *Rethinking InfoSec*, it is very much about fighting and limiting entropy so we can maintain control.

Almost everything in our framework is there to create the mechanisms and structure to fight that entropy. We define how all the things that could have an impact on security should be done, and we get the support to be able to enforce those definitions.

But there is no greater source of entropy in our battle than human beings. They can cause absolute chaos. Accidentally or intentionally.

But they can be powerful allies and champions that can not only reduce their own entropy but also spotting and rectifying deviations elsewhere. All of which helps us maintain better control over our environments.

A human factors function can make a big difference on which of those two outcomes you'll end up with.

The SecOps Domain

This domain is likely the simplest one to understand for most of the security practitioners because it's essentially what most people consider "security" to be in today's status quo.

As a CISO, I'd say it's what my Head of Security Operations would be managing. It's best delegated to an expert in security operations.

This domain is where I define how we implement, configure, run, and maintain security technologies like our general SOC setup, SIEM, EDR, Vulnerability Management, Application Security Testing, Penetration Testing, and any other non-strategic operational security activity.

That said, security operation leads should be mentored in providing as much strategic feedback as possible, and our business insights are critical to know where to prioritise operational resource.

For example, if our SOC is seeing high frequencies of certain elements being exploited, we should not just combat those attacks but also investigate the reasons behind the presence of those vulnerable elements so that they can be tackled, and their remediation planned as strategic activities.

Conversely, our business knowledge should tell us which systems, users, or processes have the highest potential business impacts and our operational security focus, or at least awareness, should have some degree of concentration there.

This is one area of security that's well serviced in terms of knowledge and as such there is plenty of knowledge out there on how to best run security operations and associated technologies.

But do remember to always keep the strategic aspects in mind to maximise their business value in addressing root causes and prioritising resource.

The Compliance Domain

A lot of organisations build their security programmes off the back of a third-party framework like ISO or NIST.

I believe this is a mistake for the simple reasons that those frameworks lack focus addressing their business's specific systems and processes.

We are far more likely to have complete, holistic, and appropriate coverage, in less expensive and less disruptive ways, by moulding a bespoke framework to our reality rather than trying to retrofit a third party's idea of security.

Especially when that "security" is mostly technical security controls with limited understanding of people and business. And *zero* understanding of *our* people and business.

That doesn't mean we shouldn't be doing compliance though. To the contrary.

We now associate "compliance" with ISO, NIST, CMMC, Cyber Essentials, etc. That's not what compliance is though, is it?

Compliance is simply the measure or process by which our reality meets its defined and desired optimal or ideal state.

That means having those definitions of what good (as in secure) looks like for everything in our environment is crucial for any effort at compliance to yield any actual security. It's why today's "compliance" rarely if ever equals security, and precisely the point of our framework and its various domains.

In short, our ultimate compliance goal is to be compliant to what we have defined in *our* framework.

We define our ideal state, for each system and business process, and comply to it. It's not just a lot easier and a better fit than trying to apply a generic control to every business process, but by instead moulding our ideal state according to *our* business we are far, *far* less likely to omit important elements or areas of our business than by basing ourselves on an external standard that has no awareness of them.

It also means that our compliance activities make more sense to others in the business as they are a direct reflection of it, which helps traction from stakeholders and increases the likelihood of that compliance being maintained.

As such, the Compliance Domain is a bit of a misnomer in the same way "compliance" is nowadays mostly a misnomer. By this I mean that my Compliance domain is actually about *third-party* compliance.

In other words: mapping our ideal compliance to what third-party standards expect.

By having systematically gone through all our business and IT processes to ensure they were secure with our programme/framework, we are quite likely to be close to 100% compliant to most of these third-party standards.

Each component of this domain is therefore a mapping of all the expected controls for a given third-party standard to where in our framework those controls or practices can be found.

If a standard requires something that our bespoke framework lacks, we can then add it to *our* framework. This means we only need to maintain one compliance programme to comply to a potentially significant number of external standards simultaneously.

We not only get better security from complying to a framework that fits our reality like a glove, but we simplify management around compliance to multiple third-party standards when our business mandates it.

Better still, becoming compliant to a new standard is often little more than a mapping exercise rather than an entire new compliance programme. This translates into more agility and opportunity for the business.
which can quickly pivot into regions or industries where additional compliance requirements might otherwise have been a barrier.

Finally, our compliance efforts are typically simpler too as the processes in our framework are themselves designed to drive the defined ideal outcome. The compliance is the process.

The Commercial Domain

Simple question: If we are the *Chief* Information Security Officers, the Grand Poobah of security in our organisations, whose job is it to handle the commercial aspects of security?

Who is responsible for creating brand value around security?

Who is responsible for answering any questions and around security during the sales process? And to improve the speed and quality with which those questions are answered?

To ensure any commitments made in contracts with customers or suppliers are captured and integrated as part of our security programme?

Whose job is it to leverage security efforts as a competitive advantage?

To make arguments that leverage security to win tenders over our competitors?

To raise public awareness of our security efforts and the resulting security of our offerings?

To develop commercial security strategies that boost our company's business?

To think about how to milk out every last bit of commercial value from the security work we're doing?

I strongly feel it's us.

It's not just a significant contribution to the business, which we should be doing anyway, but it allows us to offset the cost of the security function, sometimes beyond 100%.

It also means we have commercial discussions which cause us to be included and respected in the more commercial verticals of the business as well as with senior management.

We're even more likely to be involved into strategy and project meetings if people think we can potentially add revenue to what's being proposed rather than merely assessing its risk and potentially slowing things down.

And finally, it's a helpful connection point to Sales, Marketing, and Product departments which can be hard to reach.

This domain is one of the newest in my programmes and one of the least well established. As such you can expect a lot of variation as to what goes in this, how it can differ based on your company and what's possible, and just sheer innovation around commercialising security better.

Here's a sample of things I've put in this domain so far in the hopes of inspiring you to do even more:

- A document covering the overall commercial security strategy and related messaging and objectives.
- Shareable studies about the business risks faced by our customers, by industry or vertical where applicable.
- How we have shaped our security programme and team to address those customer risks, specifically highlighting ones they might face when doing business with a company like ours. (Which our competitors likely haven't mentioned or addressed.)
- Customer-facing documentation on our full stack of internal security practices, showing how we implement relevant security throughout the entire lifecycle of the product as well as all our business processes.
- Definition of our brand values and how security features as one of them
- Definitions on how marketing should include and communicate security messaging as part of other activities.
- Security messaging (page) on our website.
- Our public stance on security. For example: We cover the full lifecycle, we will never charge extra for security features, etc.
- Any additional blogs or campaigns we produce for internal and customer-facing security messaging.
- Extensive RFI response documentation to help sales teams accelerate the sales process by pre-emptively providing answers to security questionnaires.

- A process to ensure any security commitments in contracts are captured and implemented where needed.

I invite every CISO to put their sales and marketing hats on and really think through the nature of their business to come up with ways where security, and the perception of security, could produce a competitive advantage.

In my last CISO role I hired a former sales representative as an Information Security Commercial Officer to oversee this function. I'd argue it was a great success and it was not long before he was noticed by senior management due to his work's relevance to the bottom line.

So much so that after a change in management whereby the security function was [somewhat myopically] phased out, he was the only person asked to stay due to pressure from commercial teams. They even nearly doubled his salary.

I believe that's a solid demonstration of the impact that commercialising security can have with senior management. It's not only a good thing to do, but also hugely helpful with internal traction.

It's good fun too! It's an entirely different kind of problem solving that I greatly enjoy.

Business Stubs

The Business Stubs "domain" isn't really a domain like the others. In many ways it's a repository, or a linking point for other departments' processes.

Other departments should be able to access any relevant part of our framework documentation to ensure they know the security standards and processes we have defined.

Conversely, we also need visibility to other departments' business processes. The Business Stubs portion of the framework is a space where we can store or link to other departments' processes, inventories, etc.

This helps us have the necessary visibility over their processes, enabling us to review them for security concerns. We can potentially even have automatic alerts to any changes in other departments' processes.

I recommend structuring this section as folders, one per department, with subfolders for different functions within each.

You should ideally have a standardised way of storing business processes, like Confluence for example, that allows for easy interconnection/visibility of processes across departments.

I know this part of the framework seems superfluous to some, but I've added it to mine for a reason. Holistic coverage is absolutely key for an effective security posture and it's incredibly easy to not know about obscure business processes.

There have been many breaches of significant amounts of sensitive data due to little known processes and tools that had escaped the attention of the security department.

It also saves the respective department a whole lot of time answering a wide spread of questions from us if we have a copy of their processes that we can review by ourselves.

What we learn about the business through understanding how other departments operate (and with what data, systems, and revenue streams) should also always be in the back of our minds when we define our security processes and programme too.

Finally, when do we find issues, having this [hopefully shared] repository creates an easier way to collaborate on adjusting a given process to minimise its business risk.

Closing Off

That, in a nutshell, is how I approach building my security programmes, or at least my most recent ones.

Is it perfect? No. I keep adapting and improving it to best reflect different organisations and my own knowledge.

Could there be a fundamentally better way of doing it?

Quite possibly. And I'm perfectly happy with people thinking it's silly.

Remember that your framework is the structure to manage your programme, and your programme about delivering your strategy.

Do it any way you want, as long as there are real and sustainable outcomes in terms of improving the security of your organisation.

The important thing is to keep progressing, thinking, innovating, and not being afraid of trying something different.

No matter what your framework looks like, your ability to determine the optimal strategy and build and execute a programme to deliver it successfully will come down to the same things: Your understanding of your organisation and your leadership skills.

Appendix B – The Hitachi Vantara Blog

And now, finally, the six-part (plus introduction) blog that kicked off the idea for this entire book.

Please note that, for the above reason, there will be some overlap between the book and this blog, especially in the first instalments.

That said, I believe the instalments have enough additional content, and in some cases a different flavour, to augment some of what's come before in the book.

Most of the later instalments feature some more concrete, and hopefully very interesting, applications of the type of thinking detailed in the book.

For some background, I want to mention that one of the key motivators behind this blog was to make storage and recovery relevant to security practitioners.

I hope the ideas contained within not only help you leverage storage and recovery capabilities to improve *security* in whole new ways, but also encourage you to think of new, potentially radical, ways of using other technologies too.

Enjoy!

Blog (0/6) – Introduction

Security, Strategy, Storage, and Recovery

Welcome to this new blog series in which I will be offering a different look at storage and recovery: One from a strategic *security* point of view.

The goal is not just to better explain the relevance of storage and recovery to current and aspiring Information Security leaders, but also to introduce some concepts around "Security as Quality", what I call "Inherent Resilience", and presenting a different approach to Risk Management to help practitioners move things forward.

The reasons being that, in order to understand and appreciate the value of new approaches, it's important to understand the bigger picture and how things fit together.

I hope these insights also help IT Operations teams and CIOs realise additional security potential from platforms and processes they may not have thought as relevant.

So, what is "Inherent Resilience"? Well, it's a term I've coined to define our ability to not get knocked down in the first place. In other words: Not reaching the point of needing recovery in the first place.

I've phrased it this way because in the security field "Resilience" has come to mean something closer to *recovery* while I think our long-term focus should be focused more on not getting breached in the first place.

And if you're confused that a blog about storage and recovery is talking about avoiding the need to perform recovery in the first place, then hold on to your hat because we are going to discuss how to use your recovery capabilities to improve your chances of never needing to use your recovery capabilities. Intrigued? Stay tuned.

But first, an introduction. My name is Greg van der Gaast. I have 25 years of experience in information security. My first job was offered to me when I was 17 and some federal agents from the FBI and US Defence Department decided to make a house call. I won't bore you with the details as to why, but it involved the NSA, CIA, DIA, and some nuclear weapons. I have seen hundreds of breaches and caused a few myself - once having been labelled as one of the 5 most notorious hackers in the world.

One of my biggest observations after switching sides, was why my job as the attacker was so easy, and why what most of the security industry was doing wasn't making it much harder. As a result, I've always had what people consider a "maverick" approach to security because I believe in doing what works, long-term, sustainably, rather than the status quo.

Over the last 15 years I've since built security programmes for companies ranging from hot start-ups to Fortune 500's, lectured at universities on security strategy and leadership, advised cyber-insurance companies on due diligence (hint: quality of business processes is a far better indicator of risk than the presence of security controls), and currently assist security vendors in helping their customers get more value from their offerings.

A quick note: I am *not* a storage and recovery expert, but I want to take you on a journey to look at our security challenges, how I've tackled them, and, finally, what role storage and recovery has played for me as part of that bigger picture.

I also want to add that Hitachi Vantara, while sponsoring this series, has given me no further instructions on what to write other than helping the community at large. These are my thoughts and experiences, and I thank them for allowing me to share them with you.

But before we get started on how to develop *successful* security strategies and approaches and where storage and recovery fit in, we must look at the overall trends in our industry to see how things are going:

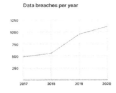
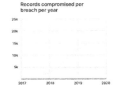
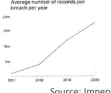

Source: Imperva

Not great, are they?

And this worrying trend is happening *despite* ever-increasing spending on security:

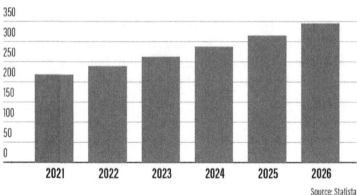

SIZE OF GLOBAL CYBER SECURITY MARKET WORLDWIDE ($ billion)

Source: Statista

In most situations, certainly at this scale and over a period now spanning well more than a decade, investment in an overall approach is expected to have an impact in reversing or reducing what it is it's trying to combat.

Instead, many practitioners, vendors, and experts use these figures to point out how prevalent and sophisticated attackers are, and that we must therefore double down further on our investment in "cyber."

I have instead come to see it as a rather damning indictment of just how poor our current approach is. Dozens of times I have seen companies with millions spent on security, with NIST and ISO frameworks in place, and still be absolutely trounced by a bored teenager with a laptop.

If we had an effective and sustainable approach to reducing issues, we should be seeing trends like those in mature industries where they too are fighting to reduce the number of incidents. They identify root causes *no matter where they are* and address them, upstream, pre-emptively.

Take the aviation sector for example, which addresses issues as far upstream as possible regardless of how distant they seem from most people's concept of "aviation" (Everything from engineering, metallurgy, corporate culture, drug use, the tone of alarm sounds, control ergonomics, human factors, etc.) to drive a reduction in possible failure points:

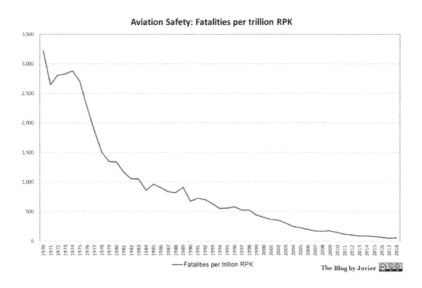

That is what the results of an *effective* approach look like.

If we found that the bolts holding the wings onto a plane's fuselage were coming loose during flights, we wouldn't set up a function where we employ thousands of people to retorque bolts after every flight, forever. We'd make a change to the design or manufacturing process *once*, then remediate what was in the field. And yet, most security work has more in common with the former than the latter.

So, what should we be doing in Information Security? It seems clear to me that a change in approach is needed. But what? And more importantly, based on what principles?

Let's begin with some opening questions:

Have you ever considered...

- That security vulnerabilities are *defects*? Whether it be in code, architecture, design, maintenance, process, or even human behaviour?
- That, to rectify this, Security might ultimately be more effective as a business *quality* function?
- Why we tend to focus on threats and protecting vulnerable applications, systems, and infrastructure, rather than on changing the business processes that lead to their vulnerability in the first place?
- If we could drive improvements to security without having to continuously (and

unsustainably) increase the scale of security operations?

- How mature industries like automotive, manufacturing, or aviation stop issues from recurring or occurring at all? And how some of approaches could be relevant to Information Security?
- Whether Risk Management could be simpler if we calculated backwards from business downtime, rather that the innumerable arbitrary compounding variables that might lead to that downtime?
- How storage and recovery capabilities can allow us to shift more resource towards a strategic security approach, rather than mitigation and firefighting?
- How recovery should be implemented to ensure reliable recovery if things do go wrong?

Over the course of this six-part series, we'll be exploring all these questions and what they mean to improving the security posture of our organisations. We look forward to having you join us for these insights. Don't miss it!

Blog (1/6) – Security as Quality

We ended our introduction to this series with several questions. Questions I've found myself asking over my 25 years working in Information Security. Some of these questions stemmed from others, and some led to more questions, but they did take me to a general conclusion:

The way that we currently practice security, overall, isn't just ineffective as shown by virtually every statistic. It's also *weird*.

We have developed very niche approaches to solving problems in our industry. But if you applied analogous practices in other industries, we would likely leave people scratching their heads at what we were doing. Conversely, other industries have developed and refined approaches that deal with analogous problems very well, yet we reject them as not applicable.

I've seen a particular Sun Tzu quote used in several security presentations talking about the importance of threat intelligence, detection, response, logging, monitoring, and a whole host of other security solutions and practices.

Know thy enemy.
Know thy self.
A thousand battles.
A thousand victories.

Most of their narratives highlighted the importance of "know thy enemy", but in my eyes failed to realise that they were omitting the *know thy self* part.

In short, I believe we are too quick to focus on the threat actors while we ignore what makes them *threatening* to begin with: Our own [excessive] vulnerability, or vulnerabilities.

But what is a security vulnerability? You could argue in its simplest form that it's a defect, a quality defect. A defect in code, in architecture, in a workflow that doesn't allow maintenance, in a procurement process that brought in something else that had defects, in any business process really. And yes, every IT process, no matter how small, is a business process to some degree.

Would we allow planes to leave the assembly line with known defects that could make them crash, and then leave it up to some "operations centre" to try and detect when these defects start causing dangerous situations, in the hope of stopping the worst-case scenarios?

The "operations centre" may play a role in detecting and trying to mitigate such an issue, but regardless of the outcome we would immediately address it in the design of the aircraft, on the assembly line, the very first time it happened, to make sure the risk is never introduced again.

At the end of most automotive assembly lines there is a person doing quality assurance. Their job is to see if any defects have been introduced in any of the 100+ sequential stations in the assembly line building the car. If they do find a defect, like the steering wheel being mounted off from centre, the car goes back to that station to be fixed. If this defect is significant or occurs more than once, then the time is taken to examine the cause and re-engineer the process *at the station where it was first installed* to prevent it from happening again.

They do not hire an ever-increasing army of quality assurance people to fix defects at the end of the line, nor would they, if a defect kept recurring, just keep sending every affected car back to the line without addressing the process that caused it to have that defect in the first place.

But these rather common-sense approaches to quality management seem to have largely escaped the field of Information Security. As a result, the more our organisations grow, the more technology we take on, the more security issues result, and the more we constantly need to firefight. I would argue that much of what we have come to call "security" has more in common with firefighting than "securing".

We are not only failing to learn from what other industries have long ago figured out, but we are also missing out on the economies of scale of putting quality into the build process (of code, systems, architecture, process, etc.) rather than endlessly rectifying things at the end. Plus, we've reached a point there the volume of firefighting is so high that we can't keep up despite forever increasing our investment in "Security".

Security is incredibly well placed and effective at detecting these quality issues, but we rarely leverage the information to actually fix the processes that cause them.

It's the reason why both incident and spending numbers keep climbing. It's the reason we too easily now say "it's no longer a matter of if but when" when most breaches have been shown to be readily preventable.

You might recall the trends below from this series' opener.

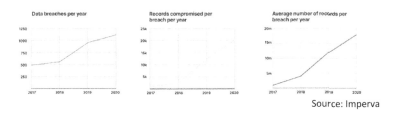

Source: Imperva

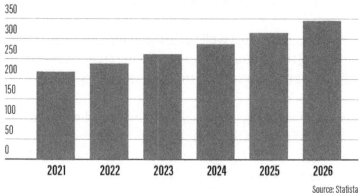

SIZE OF GLOBAL CYBER SECURITY MARKET WORLDWIDE ($ billion)

Source: Statista

Too often, security practitioners' minds focus immediately on "compensating controls" and mitigation efforts without thinking about why they are needed in the first place.

Worse still, just like every other system, the effectiveness of security controls is also dependent on the integrity of dependencies which are often not considered. For example, your IAM service validating your users cannot be trusted if it has a code defect allowing the injection or modification of accounts, or running on a server missing critical patches that allow someone to compromise it and have full control over your IAM setup.

Incidentally, this is the fundamental reason I tell cyber insurance providers doing due diligence to look at the maturity of business processes (something often primarily driven by company culture) rather than the mere presence of security controls. Without good process, the security controls themselves are likely to be ineffective or potentially compromised.

Another rarely considered and counter-intuitive angle: The needed presence of many compensating controls can point to poor business process, and higher risk, in of itself. Why were so many compensating controls needed? Why wasn't the security built in earlier? What internal issues led to that?

If a car company built a dedicated team of people to find and realign wrongly installed steering wheels at the end of its assembly line, but neither the company nor that team had bothered finding ways to make sure they were mounted correctly in the first place, wouldn't you have some questions?

Questions about the process, about the company, about the people there?

Wouldn't we be asking ourselves why they hadn't focused on the much easier solution of maybe creating a jig or a template when first installing the steering wheels so that all this work at the end wouldn't be needed? Wouldn't that be faster, cheaper, and generally more beneficial to the business?

This is my personal definition of *strategic* security. Asking the questions that lead to approaches and solutions that create long-term reductions in issues and put the business first, rather than building up operational work (with no long-term benefit) to mitigate ever-increasing symptoms of a more fundamental problem.

So, what does this have to do with storage? Or even recovery?

In some ways, not much. In other ways, everything.

This strategy, or philosophy, or *common sense,* of Security as Quality shapes how I and some others approach our roles as CISOs. It's how we strive to reduce attack surface over time, make sustainable progress rather than firefight, and lower costs. It's also a way of doing things that offers numerous additional business benefits to our organisations because improving quality improves much more than just security. Storage and recovery play a crucial role here in two ways:

The first reason is simply the security status quo that we usually start with. The common industry practices have created a "way of working" where an organisation's vulnerability is ever increasing in scale and complexity. To the point that, using present-day security approaches and solutions, that vulnerability can no longer be effectively managed with the means at our disposal. This can be seen by the trends of ever-increasing quantity and scale of breaches despite increased spending on security.

We have created a space where it's very much a matter of "If, not when." And while this phrase is technically true, in the same way that an asteroid will likely eventually hit the very spot I'm sitting in as I write this, I fear we've come to use it as an excuse to not do better.

Or we've just failed to realise there are other ways of approaching the problem.

As a result, recovery has become of paramount importance and grows more important by the day because, as the trends demonstrate, in generalised terms at least, our current approach cannot stop the breaches from coming.

The second reason is however far more compelling to me: Recovery capabilities give us a safety net that can empower us to change things for the better. It can allow us to deprioritise firefighting and instead prioritise a Security as Quality approach that drives lasting improvements.

From a pure Risk Management perspective, recovery allows us to limit the maximum impact of a breach. This means we can (and should, based on risk management logic) reallocate more resource to where it can drive greater change.

We can refocus to reducing how much risk our business processes introduce, driving long-term reductions to how much Security needs to manage, in turn freeing up evermore resource for more proactive work. This exponential growth in our power to affect change is what can turn the tide and make our organisations increasingly *invulnerable*.

That brings me to the end of this instalment which I hope has fuelled some thoughts on how we can approach security differently. In our next instalment I'd like to share how I structure security programmed and how recovery capabilities give us the freedom to reallocate resource away from reactive efforts towards ones creating long term improvements, all while helping us sleep at night too.

Blog (2/6) – Building a Programme

In this instalment I want to share with you how I structure a strategic security programme as a CISO. Both in the hopes that it can help you drive change in your own organisation(s), but also to help the practical understanding of some of the things we have discussed so far on in this series both in terms of how and why.

This will be a high-level overview at best, but something we will explore in detail in an upcoming book graciously sponsored by Hitachi Vantara.

My definition of a "strategic" or "business-level" security programme is similar to any other security or quality programme. It involves defining the ideal state of things, how we maintain that state, and capturing the necessary support and authority to do it. The real difference is the scope at which we address the problem:

Most security function and programmes focus on having the capacity to deal with all the issues the current business processes have and will produce, forever.

Conversely, I prefer to focus *primarily* on influencing business process throughout the whole organisation to continuously reduce the number of bad outputs (vulnerability, attack surface, obstacles to security maintenance activities like patching, etc.) they produce in the first place.

The first is building operational security capacity, the second is shaping the business so that things are inherently more secure and less and less operational security capacity is required over time.

So, what does such a programme look like? Well, it can take many shapes. I've evolved, sometimes radically, how I approach this over time to not just better reflect each organisation, but also to incorporate new knowledge and ideas. I hope that, should you decide to take some of the concepts and structures presented here, you also adapt and evolve them to work even better for yourself and others.

The first step is very simple: I create a framework.

I start by drawing a big square (more a vertical rectangle for me) that acts as both a box and a wireframe.

The purpose is simple: it holds everything. It's a container that everything will live in, and that will connect them all together. This overcomes the first problem I often see in organisations: discombobulated documents and policies, rarely in homogeneous formats, scattered all over the place, and with no full inventory anywhere.

Inside this box I create layers, or domains (I'll used "domains" going forward). And within these are a variety of documents. These documents can be standards, declarations, processes, policies, definitions, anything really. These are what define the desired states of things; of the organisation, of our own efforts and mandate, of our needed authority, and of the approaches we'll employ to deliver on our mission.

How many domains or layers there are can vary for each organisation, and as mentioned you should tailor this to what works best for you. But as an example, the last framework I developed for a SaaS B2B services company contained the following domains:

1. Executive
2. Programme Definition
3. HR & Legal Integration
4. IT Operations
5. SaaS & Business Applications
6. Product and Engineering
7. Human Factors
8. SecOps
9. Compliance
10. Commercial
11. Business Stubs

1. Executive: This always includes an Executive Charter that defines hard rules for security scope, responsibility, and authority, signed by the senior management team (The perfect place to pitch the security as quality concept and its many non-IT business advantages). As well as a written Security Strategy (business-centric, so well beyond IT) that explains and justifies the approach (including the framework), team structure, timelines, etc. involved in delivering it.

This is critical. You need a business security strategy, and you need real executive support. Many organisations have neither.

2. Programme: An overview of the whole programme, inventory of its components, continuous improvement process, how the activities will be scheduled and tracked.

3. HR & Legal Integration: I need to define Acceptable Use Policies enforced by HR, I need defined roles and associated access, I need HR integration for automated/effective JML, I need to work with HR and sometimes legal on investigations. All this is defined here. I also need integration with Legal for contractual reviews, certain incidents, ensuring contractual requirements are captured in IT and security service delivery, etc.

4. IT Operations: Define how we do everything IT related, from provisioning users, asset management, patching, architecture, backups, recovery, logging, email, networking, endpoint hardening, database configuration, media handling, cloud standards, change management, etc. This one tends to be quite large and could easily be broken into several sub-domains for ease of delegation or organisation. The important part is to define, in detail, with the relevant stakeholders, how each IT activity should be done with security in mind.

5. SaaS & Business Applications: Define the state in which every internally hosted or SaaS business application should be in to ensure security, one at a time, working with the stakeholders to understand the business processes, data, and potential impacts.

6. Product and Engineering: If applicable, define all the practices that should go into your product development, product security features, hosting/engineering environment, internal and external-facing product security documentation, etc.

7. Human Factors: This is where we drive cultural change (which is related only minimally to user awareness) in conjunction with HR but also work on process engineering to reduce elements of human error in business and IT processes.

8. SecOps: This is where the stuff most people think is security goes. SOC operations, EDR, anti-phishing vulnerability management, incident notification/response, threat intelligence, forensics, etc.

9. Compliance: I do not build my security according to any 3rd party compliance standard. That is not only backwards in some ways but also likely to result in missed areas and ill-fitting implementations. Instead, my compliance is based on the application of the framework. I can then easily map my security processes and mechanisms

to *any* compliance standard with minimum effort (a great business agility advantage when entering new verticals or markets). This is where those mappings happen.

10. Commercial: Here we define how we capture contract schedules that relate to security, any customer facing services like security-status portals, how we help Sales accelerate the RFI process (including any documentation to give customers), our involvement in any contractual negotiations with an impact on security, and any marketing and branding material around how our security gives us an edge. (If we think security is important, why wouldn't we have it be a brand value or selling point?)

11. Business Stubs: Links to all other departments' business processes, which should be taken into consideration when creating every component of the framework in all the domains listed above.

I typically start off building out the executive domain and getting the relevant documents approved, then create the Programme Definition layer so everyone knows how to contribute to the programme. The HR & Legal pieces (as many important other processes will depend on these) come next. Building out the rest is then mostly delegated to members of my team and collaborating other departments.

Now might be a good time to mention that, for reasons I will explain shortly, out of the dozens of activities that would fall under the IT Operations domain I always ask that the back-up and recovery piece be one of the first ones handled.

Over time, the build-out of this programme leads to close integration between departments and the involvement of those departments in security practices.

To name just a couple of examples: Access to systems can be managed automatically by HR based on role profiles and automation, systems and applications are architected and produced using templates incorporating security standards, all business processes are captured with security concerns highlighted and considered, Operational/maintenance activities like application and asset management, patching, backups, provisioning, and more become automated according to define standards, all leaving fewer gaps for potential exploitation.

The net result is greater security due to the improvement (higher quality) of the organisation's processes, not the security department's capability to firefight. This means every implemented change has a permanent effect rather than just being the latest avoided disaster.

And that is how we reverse the trend, lower the business' risk over time while needing less and less operational security resource (rather than more), save the business money, not to mention find and generate other benefits elsewhere.

I've seen everything from significant reductions in license costs, contract renegotiations, more stable applications, lower maintenance costs, higher customer satisfaction, even reduced turnover as DevOps and Site Reliability Engineers inherited fewer frustratingly hard to maintain systems. All from trying to improve the quality of processes to help, nominally, with security.

The argument of improving the business rather than "doing security" is also one I find easier to sell to executive audiences. When department heads resist, the quality argument is a powerful one. It's somewhat easy for departments to claim that it's not their job to handle security when senior leadership doesn't understand how security works. But once we've positioned security issues as being the result of poor quality, it's very difficult for those department heads to argue that they aren't responsible for the quality of their outputs.

If they insist that security isn't their responsibility, I like to ask them who they hired to lock their front door this morning.

So that, in my opinion, is the goal of a framework, and the strategic goal of the CISO.

I have yet to see anyone propose a more sustainable approach in the sense of eliminating the source of security issues in the first place.

There is however one problem with it: You must put in the work, and it takes time. Probably years.

I feel this is one reason people go for the short-term firefighting and mitigation approaches, spending most of the effort operating detection and response functions to firefight all the issues at their feet. Don't get me wrong, you need these technologies, but their greatest value isn't firefighting issues, it's giving you the end of a string to pull on to find out which business processes are responsible for the issues. We can then rectify them so that the issues stop coming, instead of spending all our time dealing with the resulting fires.

And that's where recovery capabilities come in. I know this is a radical statement to most technical security professionals, but it allows us to, in a way, let some things burn. Or rather, risk them catching fire.

We can risk them catching fire because we know we can quickly and reliably bring them all back to life, and the time saved trying to mitigate and react to every risk or threat can be spent elsewhere *fireproofing* the business processes that build our systems, applications, and define our operations. Once we've fireproofed them, we don't need to stand guard over them all the time, which is yet more resource we can shift.

That is what risk management and security leadership should be about: using the resource we have at our disposal to deliver the highest amount of value to the organisation, and to consume as little of the organisation's resources as we can. Not to "do security" in a way that we know is ultimately ineffective (as shown by the ever-increasing frequency of breaches).

In short, we know that if the worst comes to pass, apart from a confidentiality breach, things can be put back in order. And having this capability, as you work on building out your programme to be able to stop things happening in the first place, means you can sleep at night, and focus on the future during the day.

But even from a pure technical Risk Management perspective, this idea of "letting things burn" isn't radical at all in my mind. In fact, if we include the speed of recovery in our Risk Management calculations (something that obviously *should* be done but rarely is) it affects the business impact of any particular risk.

For example, one way of decreasing the impact of *all* our risks could be not to even do anything about the threats or vulnerabilities, but merely have faster recovery.

And if we increase the scope of our risk calculations to include the root causes of the risks (business process) and start looking at a longer more strategic timeline, we find that fixing the causal business process is almost always what should be prioritised. Even more so when short term risk has been mitigated by strong recovery capabilities.

And that's precisely what we'll be looking at in our next instalment: Risk Management under the light of *business* risk, how recovery time factors in, and how it helps us shift our focus to solving the root issues rather than continually mitigating the risks they cause.

Blog (3/6) – Recovery-Based Risk Management

This might just be my most controversial instalment in this series, for security practitioners anyway.

I'm going to come straight and say it: I don't like how we do "Risk Management" in Information Security. I think that in its current guise a lot of it is of very little real value, especially from a strategic or long-term standpoint.

Let me try to clarify that somewhat. As a CISO, is it is my job to "manage" risk, or to sustainably reduce how much we have and create? I prefer the latter. Long-term, it's a lot less work for me, and a lot better for the business.

I feel we too often operate with an assumption that the business wanting to do or achieve X means Y risk, but the reality is that *how* we go about doing X greatly affects Y.

In short, it's usually possible to have the outcomes the business wants with a lot less risk (and I mean before throwing a lot of mitigating security resource at it), but it involves building the business processes with risk in mind rather than retroactively managing the resulting unnecessary or excess risk.

This is something that can be done with the proactive strategies and concepts I laid out in the Security as Quality instalment.

In other words, I don't like how the security status quo has scoped "Risk Management" and the approach that is typically used for it. Together, at a macro level, they might even contribute to us staying stuck where we are; constantly "managing" new risks rather than stopping their creation and reducing the total number of risks [to manage] at any one time, over time.

In my opinion, a lot of it stems from following two things:

1. We do not approach Risk Management from a fundamental business process angle. I.e.: We do not tend to focus on changing the processes responsible for continuously generating new risks, instead only dealing with the resulting risks without reducing the flow.

    Risk Management is often a firefighting and reactive mitigation function rather than one that makes sustainable improvements to the responsible business process in the first place.

2. The fact that even in the limited scope (as per above) of status quo Risk Management, it is risk scoring that serves as the basis on which most other risk management actions are taken. This would be fine were it not for the fact that, whether qualitative or quantitative, I don't feel we're particularly good at being accurate.

    We are, as humans, often hilariously bad at determining risks and the actual causes of risks (correlation). E.g.: Pigs kill more people than sharks, cars kill more people than guns.

We also tend to simplify correlations to where A causes B, but there are often so many other factors involved that our simplified conclusion can be way off or even completely backwards. This can lead to not just poor risk calculations, but proposed actions that have little effect and can sometimes make things worse.

- Most risks are assigned arbitrary values, or even 1-5 numbers, that are disconnected from a financial business impact.

- "Quantitative" assessments, rarely are. They are still based on arbitrary assumptions that can be significantly off, whether the assessor realises it or not. I find quantitative numbers rarely consider the full complexity of the situation.

- We often lack the technical understanding of what could happen for each potential scenario. In other words, we do not know every part of every system (IPs, ports, services, operating systems, versions, installed software, patch levels, exposure windows, etc.), and all the possibilities they provide at any given time for a potential compromise.

- We rarely understand the business context and therefore actual business impact of systems. Which business process would be stopped, degraded, corrupted by a certain system being hit, or impact to another system from it, and the associated financial cost. We then need to repeat this assessment exercise for *every possible permutation* of systems being hit for any given hypothetical breach.

- There are likely many unknowns that would affect potential attack chains, leading to risk estimates being wrong by orders of magnitude. Very few are aware of every single asset of every single type they have, let alone their dependencies, interactions, roles, access profiles, what vulnerabilities they have (or could eventually have), and how that may impact lateral movement to other things.

- The state of our environment, the threat actors, and the array of exploitable situations is forever in flux. So are your risk scenarios and associated potential impacts.

- If you want to get granular, there are literally millions of potential attack vectors in even a mid-sized company. Too many to track.

- Perhaps most important of all: Good luck explaining all this stuff to a Board in under a minute!

Not surprisingly, I received strong pushback from practitioners on these views. But the fact is that in the dozens of breaches I've investigated the main cause of the breach had usually not even been identified in the Risk Register. When it was, the risk measurements, including quantitative ones, were way off.

The reality of what happened and the realised impacts (which can be counted in the aftermath of a breach) typically did not line up with what was in the risk assessment. I'm sure many readers can anecdotally relate to what I'm saying here, especially those that have suffered a breach first-hand.

In short, I don't believe our current approach is effective and I would like to propose an alternative. Let's call it Recovery-Based Risk Management.

The basic premise is this: If you've sorted your recovery procedures properly, then your maximum recovery time is a known quantity, let's say X. The business likely knows, or can readily calculate, the loss figure for X amount of downtime.

This could be calculated for the whole business or at a department or function level, but in either case you have a maximum single incident risk impact figure.

By working backwards from the maximum negative impact instead of trying to work out every possible combination of risk, threat, and vulnerability, current and future, on systems we are not fully familiar with (if at all), and about which we don't know the full impact to business, we can work backwards from that maximum impact figure and dramatically simplify the equation.

We now have a maximum impact, which should have been set within the business' risk tolerance, due to our recovery capability. If there is an incident, the threat vector used, the vulnerabilities targeted, the sequence of the attack, how many components of the business process were affected all effectively become irrelevant. We can just assume the maximum recovery time for each specific business function and associated system(s).

We don't even need to do calculations for the impact is in business (financial) terms because we can ask the business. Afterall, it's their job to know!

Importantly, this approach is also infinitely easier to explain to management, which makes it easier to get support for. Having a single maximum risk figure is also a level of detail more suitable for executive reporting.

At this point, since we've essentially capped the possible impact of incidents, the main objective becomes reducing their frequency. Something that, as covered previously, is best done at a strategic level where the aim is to reduce the amount of vulnerable surface we generate as a business, rather than endlessly ramping up the reactive capacity to try and mitigate every attack we've made possible.

I can then apply traditional score-based practices at this broader level (rather than for individual technical risks and controls) where, due to having a definitive measurable maximum impact, they work far more effectively.

For example, rather than focusing on mitigating ("managing") my, say, 1,500 most significant vulnerabilities, I can prioritise the remediation of the handful of issues in my IT and business processes that ultimately caused them.

Are most of my issues caused by bad code? Is it my architectural practices? What about my IAM? Is it all due to lacking management support? These tend to be relatively easy to answer and prioritise compared to thousands of individual technical vulnerabilities.

It only takes a quick glance at what types of vulnerabilities we have make give a usefully accurate qualitative assessment as to how many are caused by any of these root issues. And these more fundamental and less technical issues where we can use the more traditional score-based Risk Management approaches effectively because there are far fewer variables.

They make sense when dealing with a handful of broad issues, far less so with thousands of technical risks with countless potential combinations and dependencies.

To give an extreme example, in terms of total risk reduction over time, it may even be mathematically better to completely ignore all the problems we have with our current assets and only focus on the processes that will produce new systems. Afterall, the vulnerabilities we have now will age out along with the systems they are found on, and eventually disappear. But the real point is that if we do not focus at least part of our efforts on fixing the processes that lead to those vulnerabilities existing in the first place, we will never be able to decrease how many total issues we need to "risk manage."

When Italy was the kidnapping capital or the world in the 1980's, the government did something radical to stop the problem: They made it illegal to pay the kidnappers, even freezing the assets of the victim's friends and family so that they could not raise the ransom.

When this law first passed, it was not a good time for the victims that had already been kidnapped and could not be ransomed home. But kidnappings immediately became an ineffective way to make money and all but stopped.

I am not advocating that we completely stop addressing the technical issues that we have in our environments today, but rather that some of them can be left to the safety net of recovery so that we can shift resource to where it can do more strategic good. The more we shift, the fewer risks the business will produce for us to manage, allowing ever more resource to be shifted to proactive causes, accelerating the positive trend ever further.

In simpler words, the safety net of effective recovery allows us to shift resource from chasing technical problems, to fixing the business processes that produce them. To focus on the things that will have a lasting effect on lowering the curve.

One argument I hear against this approach, where we leverage the recovery safety net to "forego" firefighting to some degree in order to focus on root causes, is that when it comes to the CIA triad, it might work with issues relating to Integrity and Availability but not Confidentiality.

This is absolutely correct.

But that doesn't mean we shouldn't do it, because this "Recovery-Based Risk Management" approach can also indirectly help drive significant improvements to the confidentiality side of things.

Firstly, resource is freed due to the simplification of the Risk Management process and the lower number of risks needing mitigation (because their *impacts* have been mitigated instead through recovery). That freed resource can be refocused on issues that can't be addressed with recovery, namely those possible breaches of confidentiality.

Secondly, a solid recovery plan requires knowing where your data is. That means that as part of the exercise of setting up your recovery capability, you tend to find out where the sensitive data is located.

This not only tells you where you might need confidentiality controls, but also where you *don't*. Systems housing data subject to confidentiality concerns make up only a fraction of most environments.

In other words, while a "Recovery-Based Risk Management" approach means treating the Confidentiality part of the CIA triad separately, it helps you decrease its scope and gives you additional resource to tackle it.

So, in summary, recovery gives us some "provocative" things to think about when it comes to how we calculate risks and prioritise resource to remediate in the most effective way, for the business, and overtime. I have yet to find a way where what I've referred to "Recovery-Based Risk Management" here couldn't at the very least augment the status quo, if not improve it dramatically and I invite everything to consider what it might mean for them. I hope you'll consider it too.

And once you appreciate that, consider the advantages and changes to risk impacts of having the fastest recovery solution in the world: Hitachi Vantara and VM2020's CyberVR. More on that in a future instalment!

Goodbye for now but please join us next time when we have a look at trends in the operational resilience space, and how rapid recovery is critical to meeting incoming regulation and the associated liability. Take care!

Blog (4/6) – Recovery & Regulation

In this instalment I'd like to look at recovery from a different perspective: How it relates to corporate liability and other impacts of present and upcoming regulations around Operational Resilience and even Privacy like GDPR.

We know from GDPR that companies often fear the associated fines more than they fear the potential breach itself. It's bad enough to have a breach and experience weeks of chaos to recover (or hopefully just hours with a top-notch recovery capability), it's a whole other thing when you're later publicly investigated and eventually fined a noticeable percentage of your earnings.

Regulation around Operational Resilience, with the potential for eventual penalties, is now starting to appear in multiple countries. This means you may now be penalised for incidents that caused business downtime, in addition to Privacy fines from GDPR, CCPA, etc.

In a nutshell you'll experience downtime (losses), have to shoulder recovery costs (more losses), and then get hit by a fine for good measure (you guessed it, even more losses). That stings.

To my knowledge, the US, Europe, UK, Australia, and multiple countries in Asia, Africa, and the Middle East are currently working on regulations around Operational

Resilience. Most are, for now, focused on critical industries such as financial services and manufacturing.

Fortunately, recovery capabilities can help reduce or prevent the three areas of business and financial losses mentioned above.

Heck, it can help potentially prevent the breach from happening in the first place by empowering the Security as Quality principles mentioned in previous instalments. But in this instalment, I wanted to provide a generalised summary around the salient points of most Operational Resilience regulation, what it means to us, and how fast and effective recovery plays a role:

1. **Who is responsible for my organisation's resilience?**

    Most regulators are looking at resilience from the standpoint of the organisation and its services. It is *not* looked at from an IT-specific lens.

    It's therefore no surprise that most see the responsibility for Operational Resilience as the ultimate responsibility of the COO or equivalent.

    For example, the UK's FCA (Financial Conduct Authority) gives responsibility to what they refer to as "SMF (Senior Management Function) 24", which maps to the "Chief Operations Function". This is defined as follows:

The chief operations function is the function of having overall responsibility for managing all or substantially all the internal operations or technology of the firm or of a part of the firm.

There are however several exemptions to accountability if designated individuals have had part of the above scope delegated to them.

In most scenarios this can make the CIO accountable for the IT-relevant portions of resilience targets based on how the roles are defined to the regulator. In some cases, the CISO may also bear some responsibility, again depending on how the roles are reported to the regulator.

2. **How do regulators look at Operational Resilience?**

Most regulators I've seen use a model where acceptable thresholds are defined. These limits can vary based on industry vertical or even be self-defined. The idea being that organisations should define at what point an outage is causing unreasonable disruption to the parties dependent on their services as well as themselves (because that would inevitably impact the consumer of their services).

For example, it may be tolerable for a banking customer to be unable to access funds for a few hours, but a few days would be considered excessively disruptive. Some real-world examples of excessive disruption could include the relatively recent US FAA outage, the UK Royal Mail outage, and several UK and US Bank outages (some of which resulted in significant fines). Considering the impact these incidents had, it's no wonder regulators are keen to prevent incidents of that scale from happening.

Organisations must be prepared to meet the defined criteria for their various business activities. These must be reasonable self-defined values that in some cases need to be registered with the regulator. In some cases, the regulators themselves may define and impose these thresholds.

3. **How does *Organisational* Resilience differ from (and complement) *IT* resilience?**

When it comes to Operational Resilience, regulators are looking at *organisational* resilience and not just *IT* resilience.

While IT resilience typically supports many business processes, it's important to consider that disruption may come from non-IT failures, that the recovery of IT services may not fully restore the business process by itself, and that some business processes may not involve any IT at all.

Operational Resilience regulations' primary concern is not your IT, it is your ability to deliver services.

Conversely, switching operations to pen and paper can be perfectly acceptable from the regulator's standpoint if service levels are reasonable.

All this means that your approach to resilience, in the context of these customer-focused regulations, cannot be siloed. It must consider the full business process and all departments involved in the delivery of the service to the customer.

4. How does Cyber Insurance relate to Operational Resilience?

Cyber Insurance is a common component of an organisation's resilience strategy. It helps an organisation mitigate the financial impact of an incident by providing some coverage for expenses such as business interruption, legal fees, and data recovery costs. Its other important value proposition is that it typically gives access to expertise brought in by the insurer after an incident that can help accelerate recovery to some degree.

However, this assistance cannot be used to establish defined recovery times *before* an incident and can therefore not be relied on for defining or meeting the recovery targets looked at by regulators.

It's best to think of the insurer's post-incident services as something to mitigate unexpected situations beyond your standard recovery plan. Don't forget that there will likely also be limits in the scope of coverage and the potential risk of denied claims. In other words: Do not rely on insurance as the basis for your recovery capability, it will not tick the box.

Conversely, an organisation's existing recovery capabilities are likely to be a key factor in its ability to secure coverage, the amount of coverage the insurer will be willing to extend, and the associated premiums.

We have moved from a footing where many organisations relied on insurance to provide them with the desired resilience, to one where resilience is a prerequisite to obtaining the insurance.

In short, Insurers are more likely to cover you, for less, the better your recovery capability is.

5. **What's the best way to beat resilience targets?**

In a word: Speed.

Your recovery must be effective and complete. Meaning it must be well planned and consider all elements of business process (IT or otherwise) necessary to resume or continue operations and service delivery. This can entail restoring normal service or bringing up some temporary way of working, potentially with reduced but acceptable capacity.

Once you are confident that you have ways of restoring or maintaining your business functions, what matters most is simply how fast you can execute your recovery process. Operational resilience targets, as seen by regulators, are defined by the speed in which you can bring back service.

This means speed is *the* decisive factor in meeting targets to achieve and maintain compliance to these new regulations.

Preparation, planning, and testing are important pre-requisites. No complex recovery has a good chance of success without them. But they should be in place *before* the incident. Once a recovery needs to be triggered, it's all about how fast you can run your recovery process.

Now feels like a good time repeat something I mentioned in the last instalment: Hitachi Vantara's recovery solutions, when used with VM2020's CyberVR, have been tested as *the* fastest recovery solution on the market today.

That speed is going to help beat those regulatory targets, not to mention lower the financial impact to the business. Speaking for myself, it's an advantage I want.

6. What about forensics?

Quick story: My first encounter with Hitachi Vantara solutions was through VM2020's CyberVR solution. It had nothing to do with recovery at the time, I was more interested in the capabilities VM2020's Thin Digital Twins around security remediation and testing.

But I then saw that Digital Twins can have powerful uses in recovery scenarios as well.

I will discuss the possibilities Thin Digital Twins give us more fully in a future instalment, but I want to quickly mention one of them in the scope of this article: Forensics.

One of the biggest delays to recovery speed is the need for forensics after an incident. Traditionally, recovery cannot take place until forensics are completed. Something that can delay recovery by days, even weeks.

Due to their ability to replicate environments using only a fraction of the computing and storage resource, Thin Digital Twins allow for forensics to be done largely in parallel to recovery activities without the need to make a full copy of your environment (something most organisations do not have the capacity for).

This can save *significant* amounts of time and make the difference in meeting recovery targets, getting the business back up, and avoiding fines.

More on Digital Twins in a future instalment of this series.

To summarise, while we often look at recovery capability from the perspective of whether we *can* recover, the element of how quickly it can be achieved is often not as well considered. Careful planning and selection of recovery capabilities (technologies) and maximising their effectiveness through correct implementation and planning is key not just in minimising downtime, it's particularly crucial for meeting regulatory targets.

And that concludes this instalment which I hope helped frame what factors, both and in the future, matter to regulators and how to best meet them.

Join us next time as we take a closer look at what else Thin Digital Twins can do for us.

Blog (5/6) – Simulation for Remediation and Design

I personally feel like the field of storage has come a long way over the last 20 years. What used to be thought of mundane tape backups has potentially become one of the most innovative spaces in IT, with further innovation in solutions for cloud, virtual, and on-premises alike. Within it are some powerful opportunities for security practitioners I feel need to be better known and understood.

Today I want to focus particularly on how Thin Digital Twins can be leveraged to get so much more out of storage (and recovery). They were what started my deeper interest in storage from a security perspective. My reason for looking into them? To increase my ability to change the unchangeable.

Most security professionals are more than a little familiar with the frustrations of dealing with legacy systems, applications, and networks (we'll refer to all these as "systems" going forward). Systems for which they need to mitigate risks in evermore complicated ways due to their inflexibility, lack of built-in security, absence of support, and sometimes also a lack of documentation.

Note: Fairly new virtual and cloud-based systems are perfectly able to fall into the troublesome legacy category that we usually associate with more traditional on-prem systems if there was poor architecture in systems, applications, and process!

Worse still, legacy systems are frequently associated with fundamental (and critical) business processes. This often results in strong resistance by the business to us doing anything even remotely invasive with them for fear of disaster.

In an earlier instalment of this series, I talked about how a significant part of the purpose of a security programme is to define how things should be built so that new systems meet our security requirements. The same applies here, but for many of these legacy systems it's likely to be years before they are replaced. As a result, security teams spend vast amounts of resource adding compensating controls and managing risk around them.

But what if we could wipe out that hesitancy by the business? What if we could modify network configurations, code, system design, update software to versions we don't even know will work, do aggressive, potentially destructive, penetration testing, deploy patches with abandon, in a production environment context, all without needing to be concerned about the business impact, or even needing to go through change control?

Remediation that would take years could be done in weeks. Certainly in less time than it would take just to roll out another "compensating control" when not allowed to touch the systems, networks, or applications themselves.

Of course, the business impact and risk appetite of the organisation would never allow that. But what if there was no impact? What if the worst possible outcome of our intervention into these legacy systems didn't disrupt a thing?

The business wouldn't really care then, would they? But how would you do that? Those two things are diametrically exposed, mutually exclusive, you can't have it both ways.

Or can you? Enter the world of Thin Digital Twins.

In this article I am referring to Thin Digital Twins in the context of VM2020's CyberVR, but the general concept of general concept of a Digital Twin is a functional digital copy of a system (which can be a complex system of systems, such as an entire environments) that can be used for simulation, validation, and modelling... under the same exact conditions as the production one.

The Thin bit is the clever part and involves some really interesting patents. It allows you to functionally recreate complex systems (and whole environments) using only a small fraction of the resource.

And that's where the practicality comes in. Most organisations do not have the spare compute, memory, or storage to allocate in order to create full copies of their environment, but by using *Thin* Digital Twins it becomes possible to create functional replicas using only a small amount of spare capacity.

This means environmental changes can be tested under conditions equivalent to full production by using clones of production that replicate all environmental factors.

What does this mean to us?

Well, in the case of legacy systems, we can now generate a materially identical instance of any system (which we can pull from storage as our backups are essentially "dead" copies of our environments waiting to be brought to life) and do anything we want to them without consequence.

We can try integrating new functionality, code changes, testing the impacts of updates or patches, or even rip out a system entirely and replace it with something else to see if there's any impact to the business process. We can alter one system at a time to see if there are impacts with other replicated systems, or we can make comprehensive changes to our whole environment.

We can find out if configuration hardening changes have any negative impact on the system's needed functionality, or even aggressively pen-test "production" systems without any fear of consequence and gain insights we never could before.

In previous instalments we talked about how reactive security practices (and having to put in "compensating controls" is definitely one of those) keeps us from working on the long-term strategic changes. The kind that can sustainably improve an organisation's security posture to not only reduce risk but also reduce the cost to the business and our workload.

We discussed how outputs from business processes resulted in more and more risk to manage (and, consequently, work) due to defects caused by a lack of security thinking and integration in the creation of those processes.

If you think of removing the security defects of these processes like picking up stones on the road that are damaging passing cars, then legacy system are a bit like boulders; We can clean up the smaller things relatively easily and make sure new stones don't end up on the roadway, but the boulders can't be moved and we're going to have to do all sorts of things to keep them from causing incidents.

Thin Digital Twins can give us the leverage and power to clear these boulders, often our biggest obstacles, much faster.

They're also powerful tools for any kind of modelling of new systems, or any changes or interventions to existing systems that usually incur some resistance.

They help us prevent more from happening by enabling us to reduce existing security risks more aggressively (without us causing business risks), and better ensure that new systems aren't introducing new ones.

In a breach recovery scenario, the ability of Thin Digital Twins to replicate an environment with fractional resource allows us to perform forensics *in parallel* to recovering the full environment.

This means we can immediately proceed to recovery and then only focus on cleaning up the parts of the environment that need to be. In the past, forensics and clean-up had to happen before the recovery could run because there simply wouldn't be enough spare computing resource to run a full parallel environment.

This parallelisation of forensics and recovery saves time, and as we know, during a recovery operation, time is everything.

There's another element of parallelisation that is unequalled with the VM2020 offering. It relates to just how fast data can be pulled out of your backups.

In past instalments I've mentioned recovery times of four hours to give an example. These are not what most people would consider realistic figures due to the incredible I/O loads involved in moving data out of immutable storage. Recovery times of two to three weeks are likely more typical, though they would include several days of forensics before recovery (restoring data) was started in earnest.

So why have I been making arguments with unrealistic figures?

Well, they *aren't* unrealistic anymore, because VM2020's solution is so effective at optimising this process that in recent tests using Hitachi Vantara's Ops Center Protector the recovery of more than 1,500 virtual machines with over 100TB of data was achieved in 70 minutes.

70 minutes. Think about how being able to recover that much in such a short time changes our risk management calculations! Think about how much that limits the impacts of any risk, of any disruption becoming a major one.

Note: While those figures were achieved on virtual machines, similar performance is possible both for cloud and physical systems due to patented technology allowing CyberVR to instantly virtualise and "devirtualise" systems and apply the same process.

As mentioned previously, that makes the combination of Hitachi Vantara and VM2020 the fastest recovery solution in the world. Read for yourself using the links below the article.

https://www.hitachivantara.com/en-us/pdf/solution-profile/worlds-fastest-ransomware-recovery-from-immutable-snapshots-vmware-environments.pdf

https://www.hitachivantara.com/en-us/insights/using-thin-digital-twins-to-gang-up-on-ransomware.html

And that seems like a pretty good place for me to end this instalment. I'll leave you with a few links to find out more about VM2020 and hope you'll join me for our final and perhaps more conventional instalment where we have a look at what a good recovery looks like and how we should prepare to be able to execute it and leverage all the benefits at our disposal.

Blog (6/6) – The Importance of Recovering Well

Welcome to the final instalment of this series on how recovery can enable us to progress how we do information security.

We've seen how we can get proactive, shift focus and resource towards that approach thanks to the safety net of recovery, use Digital Twins to tackle some of our toughest legacy challenges and to accelerate forensics, what the regulatory considerations are, how speed *really* matters, and much more.

Most of these capabilities have one particular caveat though: Your recovery capability needs to be *good*. It must work well at recovering your business processes in the real world. All of them. You cannot work towards implementing a proactive programme tomorrow if you aren't confident in your ability to recover today. The distraction will consume you.

And this is where we address the more traditional or conventional aspects of backups and recovery. You may recall that one of the first things I said in this series was that I was not an expert in storage and recovery. Fortunately, there's plenty of best practices out there for us to work from.

And this being 2023, what blog wouldn't be complete without us asking ChatGPT a few things? Let's have a little fun with our favourite artificial friend and get their thoughts on recovery:

Organisations rely heavily on digital data and systems to run their operations. Losing this data due to system failure, cyberattacks, or natural disasters can have a devastating impact on the organisation's ability to function. Therefore, it is essential for organisations to have an effective backup and recovery plan in place.

Well thanks for that, Captain Obvious. So how do we achieve that? What's the process?

1. Identify critical data and systems.
The first step in planning for effective backups and recovery is to identify the critical data and systems. Not all data and systems are equally important to the organisation. Therefore, it is essential to identify the critical data and systems that need to be backed up and prioritised for recovery in case of a disaster.

Organisations can use the following criteria to identify critical data and systems:

- *Importance to business operations: Identify the data and systems that are essential for business operations. This could include customer data, financial data, inventory data, and other data that are crucial to the organisation's day-to-day operations.*

- *Regulatory requirements: Identify the data and systems that are required by law or regulation. For example, the organisation may be required to keep certain financial data for a specific period of time.*
- *Recovery time objective (RTO): Identify the data and systems that have a short RTO. RTO is the maximum amount of time that an organisation can afford to be without a system or data before it starts to impact business operations.*
- *Recovery point objective (RPO): Identify the data and systems that have a short RPO. RPO is the maximum amount of data loss that an organisation can afford in case of a disaster.*

Ok, that sounds pretty decent, applying long-established common-sense principles. Though it's important to note that just because the IT supporting a process is down doesn't mean it can't be done manually. And it's not just how quickly something starts having an impact, but how big. The $10,000,000 impact at midnight due to a failed batch job is a bigger worry to me than the $10 per minute we're losing on some live activity, for example! So do consider those things in your prioritisation. Sounds basic but I've seen this not done properly in a number of cases.

Another thing I would like to point out is how ChatGPT keeps bundling together "Data and Systems."

When it comes to backups, I would personally advise focusing on the data first as there may not be a one-to-one correlation between data and systems, then the business process(es) they're used in, then the systems supporting those processes.

When it comes to *finding* the data however, looking at the business process first is likely your best option. Experience tells me this is the best way because the business process dictates all.

That doesn't mean it may not be collecting excess and unnecessary data. But that's a separate architectural (and possibly liability) issue beyond the scope of our discussion here.

Ok, next step?

> *2. Determine backup frequency and retention period. Once the critical data and systems have been identified, the organisation needs to determine the backup frequency and retention period. Backup frequency refers to how often the data and systems are backed up, while retention period refers to how long the backup data is kept.*
>
> *The backup frequency and retention period should be determined based on the criticality of the data and systems, RTO, and RPO. For example, if the critical data and systems have a short RTO and RPO, they should be backed up more frequently and kept for a longer retention period.*

Organisations can use the following guidelines for determining backup frequency and retention period:

- *Daily backup: For data and systems that are critical to business operations and have a short RTO and RPO, daily backups should be performed.*
- *Weekly backup: For data and systems that are less critical, weekly backups may be sufficient.*
- *Monthly backup: For data and systems that are not critical, monthly backups may be sufficient.*

The retention period should be determined based on regulatory requirements and business needs. For example, if the organisation is required to keep financial data for seven years, the retention period for financial data backups should be at least seven years.

More common sense here. But again, we see the generalised mention of "data and systems" which should probably be replaced by a consideration of the business process that needs the data. In fact, ChatGPT seems to have a habit of glancing over the business putting other things first. This is a symptom of the status quo and something we need to change if we are to understand our organisations well enough to protect them.

One consideration ChatGPT hasn't mentioned is the importance of the timeliness of a specific type or subset of data. Names and birthdays may be static, but if your organisation's role is to track trends then historical data, with a full record or high enough sampling rate may also be important. This touches on the subject of full backups versus incremental ones, and the possible use of transaction to not just bring data up to date but have its full history.

Something that may also be worth pointing out is that in some cases we may need copies of data significantly fresher than one day old which is the most frequent suggested here. In fact, even minutes could be too much. Ensure you will have the data you need for each purpose.

All could require different approaches and planning to ensure we have a copy of the relevant data to support the recovery strategy for each business process.

Now we need to pick a solution (or solutions) that meets our needs and start working out and documenting the backup [and recovery] processes accordingly.

3. *Implement backup and recovery policies and procedures.*

Backup and recovery policies and procedures should include the following:

- *Backup frequency and retention period: Document the backup frequency and retention period for critical data and systems.*

- *Backup and recovery methods: Document the backup and recovery methods used, including tape backup, disk backup, cloud backup, or hybrid backup.*
- *Disaster recovery plan: Document the disaster recovery plan and the steps to be taken in case of a disaster.*
- *Roles and responsibilities: Document the roles and responsibilities of the backup and recovery team and other stakeholders.*

Backup and recovery policies and procedures ensure that the backup and recovery plan is followed consistently and helps to reduce the risk of data loss or system downtime.

After all that we should now have a documented backup and recovery process.

But how effective is it?

Next up we need to test if what we've thought up and documented will *actually work* in terms of the recovery of business processes. You'd be staggered at how few organisations have done this well or at all only to get caught out in a big way.

It's critical to define also not just how we will recover systems and data, but how the people performing the business processes will resume using them. There's nothing quite like having worked all night to get systems ready again for the business day, only to have the entire workforce twiddling their thumbs in the morning because no one knows how to start or connect to the business application as no one's ever had to do it before in living memory, it was always just "on".

4. *Test backups and recovery*
Once the backup and recovery solutions have been implemented, it is crucial to test them regularly. Testing ensures that the backups are valid and can be used for recovery in case of a disaster. Testing also helps to identify any issues or gaps in the backup and recovery plan.

Organisations can test backups and recovery in the following ways:

- *Partial restore: Restore a portion of the data to ensure that the backups are valid and can be restored.*
- *Full restore: Restore all the data to ensure that the backups are valid and can be restored to the original system.*
- *Simulated disaster: Simulate a disaster to test the recovery process and identify any issues or gaps in the backup and recovery plan.*
- *Tabletop exercise: Conduct a tabletop exercise to test the backup and recovery plan and identify any issues or gaps in the plan.*

Here I'd add to not just test the recovery solution but also the plan, including the business processes and people running them to make sure things align nicely to the business and not just the IT.

Identify any issues, adjust your plan and documentation, and retest until everything goes smoothly.

There's a slight issue that the status quo best practices don't always mention; testing this stuff is *really hard*. It's hard because it's traditionally extraordinarily time consuming, disruptive, and limited by spare resource, both in terms of manpower and computing resource.

Doing testing requires significant computing and storage resource the business doesn't likely have spare, which can result in partial and fragmented testing which may let us down in a real-world scenario. Having to do it carefully due to the associated risks also exacerbates the human effort required.

But it's another great use case for Thin Digital Twins like those leveraged by VM2020's CyberVR. Full scale recovery can be tested with far less worry. Meaning you can not only make sure you test everything, but you can test it faster and quickly reset test cycles and repeat until your recovery process is successfully proven. (Not to mention perform your forensics in parallel in the case of a breach.)

Remember that all these principles apply to all data and systems, whether physical or virtual, on-premises or cloud. While people usually assume Digital Twinning solutions only work on virtual machines, I'm glad to say CyberVR gives us options for all of these scenarios.

Remember when we said that Hitachi Vantara's Protector, when used in conjunction with VM2020's CyberVR could recover 1,500VMs with a petabyte of data in 70 minutes?

Well, I thought I'd ask ChatGPT how long it thought that would take. "Days" was the answer I got back. And once I added the elements of immutability, validation, forensics, and different elements of cloud, virtual, and physical on premise, it became "Several days or weeks."

You can see why this is exciting and a big deal when it comes to recovery. And, as a CISO, how it enables me to deliver a strategic and proactive security programme to improve my organisation's *inherent resilience* (where we don't get knocked down in the first place), thanks to the safety net and the change in priority it allows due to *Recovery-Focused Risk Management*.

Furthermore, from a from a security perspective, it's essential for your backups to be not only encrypted, but also immutably stored so that they cannot be compromised either from a confidentiality or integrity standpoint.

Another important element, that also significant impacts our ability to do Recovery-Focused Risk Management with quantitative accuracy, is how consistently we can recover from incidents (and we can even test this thanks to Thin Digital Twins).

This accuracy means we can provide more assurance to our Board and make us exponentially more likely to meet our recovery targets. It helps us not just correctly prioritise (budget) business resources for risk management according to the financial *business risk*, but also improves our ability to set and meet regulatory targets should the worst happen.

One thing I want to highlight is that there is a difference between traditional backups and the kind of recovery we have been discussing in this blog, as these differences may not be clear for security practitioners who don't live and breathe storage.

Traditional backups are great for recovering files and data, but don't provide a capability around recovering systems and business processes. In other words, they do not focus on recovering business services, which has traditionally required a lot of additional effort.

That doesn't mean traditional backups are "bad". To the contrary, sometimes all you want to do is back-up and restore files, and it is something those methods are time-tested and exceedingly good at, just keep in mind the difference between recovering critical business services and merely recovering or restoring files.

The chart below can serve as a guide which highlights and explains the differences:

Backup vs Protector/CyberVR VM20/20 HITACHI Inspire the Next

Need	Backup	Protector + CyberVR
Data protected under 3,2,1 rule to different media	✓	X
Long term retention of data (months/years)	✓	X
File/object indexing and restoration	✓	X
Immutable data protection at the lowest level (hardware)	✓	✓
Predictable and proven RTO of 100s-1000s of VMs/TB	X	✓
End-to-end recovery automation (storage/compute/network)	X	✓
End-to-end recovery of 1000 VMs	??	< 1hr
Virtual-air-gap recovery for ransomware containment	X	✓
On-demand FULL test/dev environments for DevSecOps	X	✓

Some parting words to my fellow security practitioners in this, the final instalment, of this blog:

Like me, most of us are not experts in storage and recovery. But we must accept and appreciate that it is a highly complex discipline, likely rivalling that of security.

This instalment only covers the utmost basics, and I would recommend leveraging expertise from specialised consultants (such as those at Hitachi Vantara), due to the experience and expertise needed at a business and IT operations level as well as in terms of the degree of product and technology knowledge needed to get it right.

But whether we use internal or external expertise to get it right, once it is we gain immense possibilities in changing how we do Risk Management, and how we can approach the work of securing and reducing the risk to our organisations. Moving away from mitigating and firefighting technical issues caused by business processes (including IT), to instead affect those processes themselves, building security *into* them rather than adding it to them wherever possible, and creating sustainable improvement in our organisation's security posture similar to the trend we saw in the aviation sector in this blog series' introduction.

As technology becomes ever more important in everyone's lives, we have an opportunity to make a *lasting* mark, one that truly matters.

Thank you for reading.

Printed in Great Britain
by Amazon

33758548R00155